Books by Mary Catherine Campbell

Prince of Cwillan

Forest Lake

Tomorrow Is A Long Time

The Golden Coin

Prince of Cwillan..."A very intriguing book
with unexpected twists"...Mary Ellen

"From the desert of Arizona to the old sod of
Ireland, 'Prince of Cwillan' is a journey into a
fantasy adventure, romance, and tales of
another world you will not want to end.
Getting to know the characters and their lives
is like meeting old friends for the first time. I
can't wait to continue the journey!...Judi F.

The Golden Coin

Book Four In the Prince of Cwillan Series

Mary Catherine Campbell

ISBN: 0988360950

ISBN 13: 9780988360952

Library of Congress Control Number: 2014914043

Thistle And Shamrock Publishing, Shelby Township, MI

Book Four

In The Prince of Cwillan Series

Heroes Return

Six will go though the portal with you.
Only five will return.

One, who you once counted as friend,
will turn on you.

Take care, evil is in the wind,
where it lands there will be trouble.

Brid

Prologue

Lonán waited in the hall with the other young men who had not yet moved from Apprentice status to Guardian, nor joined the High King's personal guard. Ruadrí was here as well, no longer the Leader of the Youths, he was now one of Feargus' trusted men.

Below in the courtyard, Lonán had passed Lun Dubh on his way to the stables. It was strange, even though Lun Dubh was good, even great — he had bested Lonán's younger brother Dobailein, had bested many of the young men here today — yet he never rose above Apprentice. Though now Lun Dubh called himself a tracker.

Lonán only talked to Lun Dubh when necessary. He forgot all about the tracker when the door to the anteroom opened. It was here that their Ard Ri, Feargus, gave private audiences.

All the young men came to attention.

Lord Rónán stepped into the hall, spoke with Ruadrí, and moved to where he was able to look over the Apprentices. He nodded at Lonán, "Follow me." To the rest of the young men he said, "You are dismissed."

Lonán entered the ante-room.

He had never been in this room before. It was a small but well appointed room that befitted Feargus' status as High King. Beautiful tapestries hung on the walls. There was one depicting the Judgment Tree, the others were of familiar scenes around Cwillan.

Feargus sat upon a high-backed chair. What caught Lonán's attention more that the furnishings was a gold coin that lay on the table to Feargus' right.

"Are you sure he can deliver this message?" Feargus asked.

"Yes, lord," Ciarán said. "I know the way, and can instruct him."

"Lonán, step forward."

Lonán did as the High King commanded and waited.

Feargus picked up the gold coin, placed it in a velvet pouch and placed that into a bigger, older looking leather pouch. "You will take this coin and put it in the hands of Cullan Donal," he said, as he tossed the pouch at Lonán. "He will understand the message."

Pleased, Lonán caught the pouch and smiled. Then it came to him what Feargus was asking him to do. The smile slipped from his face. He forced himself to stand taller; to fail now would mean never becoming a Guardian like his father.

"Vél will take you into the Fásach Mór," Ciarán said. "May The Father watch over you."

CHAPTER ONE

At Forest Lake, Donal was surprised that the cameras he had turned on before he went to Cwillan were turned off. In fact all the cameras were now off.

He pulled out his estate-linc and keyed in Martin's number. It only took a second before his foster son answered.

"Do you want me to come up to the house?"

"No. I was wondering why all the cameras are off?"

"I left the computer on the day I passed out at your desk, perhaps someone else turned them off. I think one of the Ladies called Mánus."

"Thanks, Martin. I'll talk to them."

Donal turned the estate-linc off and walked into the kitchen through the back hall. Alvin was sitting at the huge wooden table drinking tea. As soon as Donal entered, Sally Brown took down a cup and poured tea for him. This was an opportunity for him to question Alvin about the bunny.

He sat down across from Alvin.

After adding sugar and stirring his tea, he said, "Do you know what happened to Fionn's bunny?"

Alvin looked up surprised. "No, nothing. The poor little thing just died."

The baby rabbit had been very small. Perhaps that was all. It was just too small to survive.

"Do you know where Mrs. Murphy is?" Donal asked Sally Brown.

"She is up with Moya. Is there something I can help you with?"

"I just wanted to ask her if she knew who turned off my computer the day Martin became sick in my office." Out of the corner of his eye he saw Alvin look up, as if something had startled him.

"I think Mrs. Murphy did. I can send her along as soon as she comes down."

Donal reached for a scone. It was cinnamon raisin, his favorite; he took his time eating it. When he was finished he stood. "Alvin, you must have work below".

Alvin gulped down the last of his tea and stood.

"It is always so cozy here; I tend to forget the time." He picked up a scone and turned and hurried out the back door.

Later, Mrs. Murphy knocked on Donal's office door and entered without waiting for him to call to her to come in. It was not like her to knock and walk in; she looked uneasy.

"Sally said you wanted to talk to me."

Donal stood, "Please." He motioned toward the living room section of his office. "Can I get you something, a glass of wine or Baileys?"

"I'm fine," she said sitting down. "It won't be long now, before the baby comes."

"No, it won't. We are both hoping for a girl. But as long as the child is healthy, boy or girl, it won't matter." Donal paused. Mrs. Murphy sat on the edge of the couch with a balled up hanky in her hand. Why was she so nervous? "You called Mánus the day Martin became sick. Was anyone else here?"

"You know, I don't like telling tales out of school..."

"But?"

"Fionn came to get us, Sally and I. We called down to Carl. He wasn't feeling well either. He said to call Mánus." Mrs. Murphy paused before she said, "The ambulance came immediately from Prescott..." she paused again.

"And?"

"When we came back into the house after seeing the ambulance off and closing the gate again, I noticed that your office door was slightly ajar. To make a long story much shorter...Alvin was in your office."

"Any idea what Alvin might have been doing?"

Mrs. Murphy shook her head. "He was brazen enough to sit at your desk. I reminded him he wasn't allowed in your office. I hope I didn't mess up your computer."

"You turned it off?"

"Yes."

"Don't worry about it, you didn't mess anything up," Donal said, giving her a reassuring smile.

When he was alone, Donal turned on his computer. What had Alvin been doing? Was he trying to find or delete something?

Nothing seemed different except that all the cameras were turned off. Why? Donal was about to turn the laptop off when he noticed down in the left hand corner, almost completely off the desktop, the edge of a folder. Perhaps this is the folder that Martin made. He caught the edge of the icon, moved it to the center of his desktop, and double clicked it.

Is this what Alvin was looking for? Or perhaps he was trying to delete it and in his hurry missed the trash basket. A date check showed that it was the folder Martin had made that day.

Donal had almost gone through all of the sub-folders before he found what Alvin was looking for. It was damning evidence. He would have to call Mánus, but first he needed to check a few things out.

Both his son, Rónán, and Martin would be happy to know they might have discovered the person who had made them sick.

CHAPTER TWO

Donal waited until Carl, Devlin, and Alvin were eating dinner in the kitchen. Earlier he told Sally
Brown to take her time, keep them in the kitchen as
long as possible, especially Alvin, and to call him when
they left.

Down in the studio building Donal and Martin
entered Alvin's room.

"I found the shoe box up in the studio kitchen
where you said it would be. I left it just as it was, after
taking a small sample. He won't know we are on to him.
Though, I'd like to ring his scrawny neck for what he
did to Rón and me."

"Also Carl, and it looks like Jenny too."

"Jenny? Do you think it was his fault?"

"I hate to say so, but it looks that way."

Donal remembered the strange aftertaste of the
tea Alvin had given Rónán. It would be a hard thing
to prove, but it sure looked like Jenny had been given

the same tea that made Carl, Rónán, and Martin sick. Perhaps the tea combined with meds had set her off.

"Let's see what we find in his room."

Donal took the dresser. Martin went over to the closet.

"Do you think we are going to find something here?" Martin asked.

"Yes. I think he has gotten over-confident."

"Nothing on the floor among his shoes or boots." With care, Martin checked the clothing, trying to keep everything just as he found it. "Nothing on the top shelf but blankets."

Martin moved over to look under the bed.

As Donal closed the last drawer a memory from long ago came to him. It was Niall finding the vials under the blankets in the cabinet in his room.

"Did you check under the blankets?"

"Yes, but I'll check again." Martin walked back to the closet. He was tall enough that slipping his hand under the blankets was easy. "Damn, I must have missed this." From under the blanket he pulled a manila folder. "It was pushed to the back corner. You're going to want to wring his scrawny neck too."

Donal took the folder from Martin. Inside he found newspaper and magazine clippings. There were cut out letters, others were whole words. There was also blank writing paper and envelopes.

Donal slipped out his estate-linc, keyed it to camera, and took photographs of the contents of the folder. Martin placed the folder back under the blankets.

"I'd like to do more than..." Donal said, as he turned off the camera and was about to put the estate-linc away. He stopped. His estate-linc vibrated. He checked the caller. "It's Sally. Let's go."

They hurried out the back door.

CHAPTER THREE

At Askeaton the next day, Cathal O'Brien, Mánus Scanlon's Guardian, stood and moved over to the bar. He picked up a pencil lying on top. He was so angry; he snapped it into two pieces, as if it were a straw.

"Take it easy," Mánus said.

Cathal threw the pencil away and sat down again. "I knew he was a thief, but I never expected something like this. Donal and Martin will have to get in line behind me to punish Alvin."

"We need to talk this over with Donal. Moya is due sometime next month. We'll go over to Forest Lake when it is closer to her due date."

Cathal sighed.

"It is best to keep this between us," Mánus said. "It will break his mother's heart, when she finds out what Alvin has been playing at all these years. Seán has someone keeping an eye on Michael O."

"Wait until Liam finds out."

"Your father isn't well, for now I'm not going to tell him either."

Cathal nodded.

"If you talk to Alvin, be careful, we don't want to let him know we are on to him."

CHAPTER FOUR

Donal, his son, Rónán, Martin, Mánus, and Cathal, were sitting in the living room section of his office at Forest Lake. They were waiting. Earlier, Mánus had commented that Seán had a helicopter standing by just in case.

Now hours later, no one said a thing, the time for talking was over. Moya's labor had gone on too long and Donal was worried. In the world he came from woman died during childbirth more often then here. He had to remind himself that she had excellent care. He almost jumped off the couch when the knock came at the hall door.

"Come in," he called.

Mrs. Murphy with Sally Brown in tow stood in the doorway.

Donal stood, "Is she all right?"

Mrs. Murphy tried hard to keep her face straight and failed. "It's a girl," she said with a big smile. "The doctor will call down when you can go up and see your daughter and Moya."

"You can relax, everything went well," added Sally Brown. "Mother and baby are fine."

Everyone stood up, talking at once and congratulating Donal. Rónán hugged him and said he was happy to have a little sister, someone to be friends with his little girl.

Martin served a round of twelve-year old Jameson whiskey. Rónán lifted his glass and said a toast to his father, stepmother and his new sister.

"Have you a name for the little one?" Mánus asked.

"Yes. Fionnuala Mór, after her mother and her foster mother," Donal said, pleased that he had a daughter. Feargus had been wrong. Spring was a good time to have a girl-child.

 ❧

That evening, Donal stepped outside into the cold night. It had turned unseasonably cool for this time of year. He walked out to the top of the stairs that went down to the stables. It was late, but he couldn't sleep. He was too excited about his baby girl to relax. Alvin was on his mind too. He looked up into the vaulted sky with thousands of twinkling stars.

"Thank you," he said out loud. He touched his forehead, then his chest. He was always closer to the Father outside in the natural world.

He was about to turn and go back inside when out of the corner of his eye he saw a flash in the night sky.

Shooting star. I can make a wish for my little girl.

When the next flash came, arching up into the sky, and falling to earth as it flamed out. Donal turned and hurried back inside the solarium, leaving the sliding door open.

In the bottom drawer of the first cabinet, next to a first-aid kit he pulled out a wooden box. From the box he took out a Very Flare Gun, checked that it was loaded, took out another cartridge and hurried outside.

Donal waited for the next signal.

When it arched up into the sky. He walked to the top of the stairs, pointed the gun out and up, he pulled the trigger. When the flare died he waited. Minutes later another flaming arrow pierced the sky. He rammed another cartridge into the gun, lifted it up and fired again.

After the flare died out the night sky above the island remained dark.

Donal pulled out his estate-linc and punched in Martin's number. He didn't have long to wait.

"Martin here."

"I need you. We just had a signal from the island. Bring a backpack and one of those micro-fiber blankets."

"I'll be right down."

Donal went inside and closed the sliding door.

From the refrigerator under the microwave he took out several bottles of water, he lifted the glass top off the footed cake stand and took out half a dozen scones. He wrapped the scones in a clean kitchen cloth. He left everything on the table and walked down to his office. After turning the alarm system off he took out his dagger, slipped the sheath onto his belt, and hurried back to the solarium.

He was putting the flare gun away when Martin joined him.

"Who do you think it is?"

"No way to tell," Donal said, as Martin slid his gun into the holster and slipped his jacket on.

Seeing Donal watching him he said, "I would rather be safe then sorry. I can't get that man you were telling me about out of my thoughts."

"Lun Dubh?"

"I wonder if he followed you and saw the portal last fall."

"We will find out soon enough."

They both almost jumped when someone tapped on the glass door. Through the tinted glass it was impossible to tell who was out there. With caution, Martin opened the door.

Devlin slipped in with only a shirt and jeans on.

"You asked me to keep an eye on Alvin. He is gone. I though you would want to know," Devlin said in Irish.

"How do you know that he is gone?" Donal asked.

"I heard someone on the next level, and then the door closed. I was curious and went to check. His room is empty."

Donal was angry with himself for not dealing with Alvin sooner. He should have dealt with him back when he threatened Fionn. Telling Mánus would have to wait until the morning, he didn't have time to deal with this new problem. He was about to send Devlin back to bed.

Then thought better of it, three men would be better than two.

"Go get your jacket and boots, meet us at the garage."

Devlin didn't comment, he turned and hurried back down to his room.

～

Devlin stood guard near the knoll, while Donal circled one way and Martin the other. When Donal was in position he whistled the opening notes of "Girl from the North Country" and waited. The answering whistle was an up trill, then down again.

Satisfied that Martin was in place he stepped from the shadows into the light created by the small fire, where a man sat head down, dozing.

"I saw your signal," Donal said in Irish. Until the man stood, Donal had no idea who he was. "Lonán! Are you alone? Is your father well?"

"Lord, yes and yes. I thought you would wait until morning."

Donal signaled for Martin.

"Who brought you?"

"Vél. He waits on the other side, across from the stairs. I came during the light, but waited for dark to signal you. I signaled earlier, waited and decided to try again."

"Tell your father you have done well."

"Thank you, lord," Lonán said, sketching a bow.

Martin stepped into the light.

Lonán shivered, and moved closer to the fire.

"Martin the blanket."

Martin unfolded the blanket and wrapped it around the younger man. He also pulled out the scones wrapped in the towel and a bottle of water from his backpack.

Lonán took the scones and wolfed down two. "I will save the rest for Vél." He stared at the bottle Martin held out to him, took it and turned it over as if he didn't know what to do with it.

"Sorry, I forgot." Martin said. He took it back and unscrewed the cap and handed it to Lonán.

Lonán eyes grew round as he stared at the strange bottle that gave a little under his fingers.

Donal made a motion with his hand. "It is only water."

Lonán tipped the bottle up gulped down half of it before he lowered the bottle again and stared at it. He squeezed it several times before saying, "What magic is this?"

"Just a water bottle." Donal said. He would remove these strange experiences from Lonán's memory before he went back through the portal. "What brings you all this way, son of my friend?"

With his free hand Lonán fumbled under the blanket and produced an old pouch. "Feargus sends you this," he said, handing the pouch to Donal.

Donal took the pouch and moved away from the fire. From the weight and feel he knew what was inside. At the edge of the lake he stopped and took the gold coin from the velvet pouch.

He remembered the day he gave it to Feargus. His son had just taken the throne of Cwillan at only fifteen or sixteen. Though young, Niall had prepared Feargus for the day he would become Ard Ri.

Donal remembered the words he spoke that day.

"If ever you need me, send this coin to me."

"And how would I know how to find you?" Feargus asked.

"Ciarán knows how to find me."

Donal cleared his head; there was so much to do. Mánus would have to deal with Alvin. Donal turned and walked back to where Martin and Lonán waited for him.

"Time is short," Donal said. He had done the math as they drove out to the island. "You must go back soon."

"What message should I give Feargus?"

"Tell him I am coming." Donal paused, in his head he was going over everything they would need to do. "Tell Vél I will need several horses and half horses to use as pack animals. Also tell him to watch for me, I will come as soon as I can, at the latest expect me around Lúnasa."

"Yes, lord. I will tell Feargus."

CHAPTER FIVE

At Avenue Three in Boston, Robert Tolan absently nodded as his drink was set down on the table. All his attention was focused on his tablet. When he sensed that the person was waiting, he looked up surprised to find Mánus standing there.

When was the last time he saw Mánus Scanlon? Was it at Jennifer Tolan's funeral? It seemed longer than that. Mánus still dressed like an advertisement in a men's magazine.

"This is a pleasant surprise," he said. It was a lie and they both knew it. His next thought was, *what does he want with me?* "Please, join me. Have you had lunch? The mussels here are fantastic."

"I don't eat this early," Mánus said, as he sat down.

Robert glanced around. "Where is Cathal? How is he doing?"

"He's fine, busy as ever. I hope you don't mind me showing up like this."

"Not at all, Uncle."

"Funny, Rob. You haven't called me that in years. You stopped even before you went to college and shortened your middle name to an initial."

Robert ignored the comment and signaled his server to bring another glass of Midleton. How had Mánus found out where he had lunch?

"Is this a family visit, or are you going to propose business between my father's company, MSS, and the Robert Long Agency?"

"Just a visit. Your father manages all business between MSS and the agency. Your secretary told me where you were. Don't be hard on her. I told her I was your uncle and only in town for the day."

"There isn't a woman born that you can't charm."

The server brought the drink.

"Sláinte," Mánus said and took a sip. "Begorrah, you have good taste in your choice of the creature."

"You can drop the old-sod routine," Robert said. "Or is it called stage-Irish now?"

Mánus took another sip of his drink, put the glass down and said, "Come home."

Robert was surprised. He hadn't expected the direct approach.

"Why?"

"Your father misses you."

"Really?" Robert didn't put much conviction into his voice. "When my father retires, my younger brother Rónán can take over."

"Rónán will never become taoiseach. He is studying to be a doctor."

"Well," Robert said. "Don't look at me."

"Your twin and you are safe. I'm not sure when you stopped believing. Sometime after you became a teenager? Or perhaps it was after your fight with Jason Strickland in high school? You have to at least believe in what we stand for."

"I never believed. My father is fine without me. If he were so concerned he would have come himself."

"You forget, he didn't kick you out. You walked out through your own choosing, but you never understood anything about your father."

"Oh, but I do. My father is all about money, and his crazy beliefs. I think you wasted a trip out here, Mánus. I am not coming home. Get Martin to take over."

Mánus gave him a shocked look.

Too late Robert thought, *I put too much anger into my comment about Martin.*

"I never knew that you had so much anger toward Martin. Too bad, Rob Niall. You really should come home."

"My name is Robert."

"Come home before it is too late, lad."

Surprised again, Robert said, "Has something changed?"

"Life changes all the time."

"Having one of your premonitions, Uncle?"

"What are you so angry about?"

"I could have been an Olympic runner. Donal's feud with Strickland ruined that for me."

"Really?" is all Mánus said.

"Yes, really," Robert repeated, his voice rising in anger.

"You were never going to be an Olympic runner, Robert. And you know it. You're too lazy. Olympic athletes get up at dawn to train before going on to school or to their job. Then train again when they are done. When was the last time you had that kind of dedication?"

Mánus took a sip of his drink. "Was it just a line to impress the girls? Did you pray on their sympathies in college crying about how you could have been a world-class athlete? Did you make your limp seem a bit worse?" There was anger in his voice now. "Did they catch on? Is that why you dropped out?"

Robert fisted his hands. He wanted to hit Mánus more than he had ever wanted to hit anyone in his life.

"Don't even think about getting violent. Your father isn't here to protect you. You'd end up being very, very sorry."

Robert was taken aback by the comment. Growing up it had been rumored that Mánus could read minds. He hadn't believed it as a child. He didn't believe it now. It was just a lucky guess based on body language, nothing more.

Mánus finished the last of his drink and stood. "Come home before it is too late," he said. "As it is, it might be too late already."

Robert was left sitting in the restaurant. He felt more alone in that moment than he had since his mother's accident. He wished he could call Susan, or stop by and talk to her.

He sighed; he had burned that bridge a long time ago.

There was no going back.

CHAPTER SIX

In August, the Great Desert was still hot, but soon the weather would turn cooler as winter took over the land. As the sky above turned from salmon pink to blue streaked with silver, Donal approached the cut in the rocks that led to the only watering hole in the western side of the Great Desert. How Déaglán had found it was a mystery to everyone. Without it, he and his whole clan would have perished here in this lonely hot place, their bones left to bleach in the relentless sun.

Two summers back, after a windstorm near the western portal Donal had found the remains of two small children. How many never made it to the Valley of Fire? As a youth he was told that Cuilin, Déaglán's youngest son, went east and was never heard from again. His homeland, Cwillan, had been named after the lost son, though the spelling and pronunciation had change over the years.

He thought about Robert and why his son had joined their small party. His son was looking for redemption, Donal hoped he would find it.

He had been surprised when Robert's car pulled up next to him at the mailbox on the county road. His son signaled for him to get in. Donal closed the mailbox and locked it.

"I thought getting the mail was one of Martin's duties?" Robert said, as Donal settled himself in the passenger seat.

"I needed to get some exercise."

"You?" Robert said. "You look barely older than the day I left home."

"So you admit you left home."

Robert frowned at his father, but said nothing.

"This is a real surprise, Rob. No one to fight with in Boston?"

"Sorry, I got carried away in the hotel room last week."

"Apology accepted." He didn't want to go over the fight. Rob had screamed so loud that the people in the next room had called security. Donal watched Rob for a minute before adding, "Nothing has changed."

"We need to talk."

"My Trust and Will stay the same. It has nothing to do with you. Actually, I changed it right after Fionnuala Mór was born."

"You will be mystified about why I am here," Robert said, as he pulled the car up in front of the house. "Before we go in I need to talk to you, without my brother or Martin around."

"Okay," Donal said, as he turned to face his son. "How much do you need?"

"This isn't about money," Robert said, anger in his voice. He stared out the windshield for a minute before he turned and said, "I want to go with you."

"Go where?" Donal said, wondering how Robert figured it out.

"When we talked in Boston I noticed that you needed to get a better hair stylist and a shave."

"I always wear my hair longer then what is the current style."

"I thought about it a long time, put two and two together and came up with five. You're going back and I want to come with you."

"How can I go to a place you don't even believe exists?" Donal asked his son, then he shook his head. "I can't believe this." He looked up as though he were speaking to the Father, "Surely there is a better sixth than this."

"What?"

"Never mind. Go on."

"I lied. I calculated the timing of the portal and went there when you were out of town. I know it exists and I want to go with you."

At first Donal became angry. Why had his son said those terrible things the day he left home if he knew Cwillan was a real place? He calmed himself and said, "I don't believe you."

"When you pass through the portal it is like moving through liquid air. On the other side you find yourself standing on one huge flat boulder. At the end of the boulder are huge rocks that form a stairway down to the canyon floor. There is nothing to the east or west, nothing but desert."

Donal didn't know what to say. Robert had always been good with figures. In some ways he was a lot like Feargus, his older brother.

"You're not a good rider, you don't speak the language and most of all you don't understand the seriousness of why I'm going back. I could be gone for months or years." He didn't add, *I might not come back at all.*

Brid's words came to Donal: "*Six will go through the portal with you. Only five will return. One, who once counted himself friend, will turn on you. Take care, evil is in the wind, where it lands there will be trouble.*"

"I have to go. To prove to myself, and everyone else, that I can stand on my own two feet. Whenever grandfather talks about Uncle Billy he always says he must be a throwback from his late wife's side of the family. I know he says that about me when I am not around."

"Did you tell your grandfather and Donald?"

"I told grandfather. He said I could take a year off, but not to come back, unless I planned to make some serious changes in my life. I'll talk to Donald tonight."

Donal thought about the sixth, made his decision and said, "Drive the car down to the garage and park on the side. We'll go in through the solarium."

At the house, Donal paused, with his hand on the handle of the glass door, he turned to Robert. "Are you sure about this?"

"Yes, more sure than anything I have done in my life."

Donal slid the glass door open and let Robert go in first. Martin and Rónán were sitting at the table going over paperwork. Devlin and Fionn were over by the coffee maker talking.

"Gentlemen," Donal announced. Everyone looked up. "We have our sixth."

Donal didn't want to continue with the memory, to think about his last night with Moya and his daughter. It would only sadden him. He pulled himself back to the present.

He climbed up into the v-cut in the rocks. At the top he stopped to look at the oasis hidden in this saucer-shaped valley that ran back to a high rock wall from which life giving water flowed down to form a small pool. No matter how often he saw this view he was always amazed.

He whistled an up trill, then down and waited.

The answering trill came.

Seconds later Lonán came running down the valley. They embraced. Donal noticed that Lonán wore a gold ring on his right hand showing he was now a Guardian.

"I am glad to see you are alone. I have much to tell, news from my father, lord."

"My foster sons stayed with my sons, with our supplies."

"Come, we will talk up in the cave."

Donal followed Lonán up the valley, to the right of the pool they climbed up onto a rock shelf. Lonán had set his camp up in a small cave. Over a breakfast of honey-water and bread they talked.

"The half horses are below with my horse. Vél sent many, unsure of how many you would need. He will wait for us at his holding."

"I thought that Vél would meet us here."

"Feargus thought it best that Vél meet you on the eastern edge of Cwillan. You can use my horse tonight, or I will meet the others for you."

"I thank you for the offer of your horse, but I will walk the pack animals back to the portal. You will need a fresh horse to return to Cwillan." Donal finished the last of his bread. "What news do you have of what is going on?"

"It grieves my heart to have to tell you, lord..."

Donal waited.

"It started in the winter. Due to the drought, food was short. Some of the lords thought that Feargus should take care of the shortage. Where they thought he could come up with food is beyond me. He gave what he could. He also sent Tole and our good abbot, Tuathall, to speak with Owayn II of Wyneth.

"Soon a rumor from the south came that Feargus is not our true Ard Ri. They said the Father was punishing us because he took what was not rightfully his."

Donal was stunned; it was an old belief about a bad harvest being the king's fault. Their pagan ways had changed when Pádraic brought them the true religion of the Father and Son. How would these same thankless lords like it if Feargus invoked the old ways of the king and his retinue wintering with them at their holding?

For a minute Donal was at a loss for words. Finally he said, "The old ways die hard. Do they question his birth, my marriage to his mother?"

Lonán looked surprised.

"You did not know?"

"No, lord. Feargus always said you were a lord who lived on the eastern side of the White Mountains. Kin to him and a close friend to my father." Lonán paused, realization dawning in his eyes. "Then that means that you are Prince Cullan."

"I go by Cullan Donal now. This is Feargus' kingdom, not mine. I thought that Feargus would have told you when you became a Guardian."

"I do not know what to say."

"Prince Cullan has become a legend now, few if any know who he was, or what he looked like. It is a secret only known to a few friends. And for as long as possible, I would like to keep it that way."

Lonán nodded agreement.

Donal sat back to think about what Lonán had told him.

This was worse than any of the things Donal imagined when he received the golden coin. Feargus would not give up the throne, he held it for his son, Fintan, and his son's son after that.

If Feargus weren't High King, the throne would revert back to Niall, or himself. Both of them would be branded as part of the conspiracy. Their lies about Donal's identity would have to be made known. Many would not want to follow either of them. Though there were some who would be loyal to the throne, regardless of who sat on it, there were men devoted to Feargus and would not agree to a change.

This threatened everything Feargus and he had worked for all these years.

It meant civil war.

CHAPTER SEVEN

As Donal packed his supplies, he glanced back at Rónán who was helping Robert pack their half horse.

Across from him Martin said, "Do you think Robert will be all right?"

"I hope so. I'll keep the pace down. We need to start out before dusk. I also need someone to help him."

Donal looked over at Martin, who busied himself with his work, then over to Fionn and Devlin. Devlin put his head down, pretending to be busy tying a knot.

Martin stopped working on the load they were tying down. "I should have knocked him down that day he said those terrible things to you."

"Perhaps I should have too," Donal said.

He didn't really believe it. It would have been just one more thing for Robert to complain about. He didn't blame Martin's feelings toward his son. Robert was lucky that Donal had been able to convince his grandfather to give him and his twin a job when they dropped out of college. What would have become of the twins if Robert Long had said no?

"I'll help him," Fionn said.

Donal smiled at his youngest foster son. "Go raibh maith agat," Donal said. "Thank you, son of my heart."

"Are Mánus and Cathal going to handle the problem with Alvin?" Martin asked, changing the subject.

"Yes," Donal said. "They have brought in someone that Alvin doesn't know and hope to resolve the problem soon."

∾

Robert Tolan watched Donal and his three foster sons as they loaded the tent poles onto a mule, which for some strange reason they called a half horse, and strapped them in place. When that was done they strapped the walls and top of the tent to the next two mules. He was impressed that Donal could keep up with the younger men.

"I could use a little help here," Rónán said.

"Sorry," Robert said to his younger brother. "Do you think it is hot here all the time?"

"This is nothing," Donal said joining them. He checked their work. "It is worst from May to mid August. It is actually getting cooler."

Donal helped them pack the last of their supplies.

When his father moved on, Robert looked over at his brother. "Why did you come?"

"I came because our father needed me."

Robert saw the glint of gold on Rónán's hand. He reached over and caught his right hand. "I see why now. When did you join the brotherhood?"

"Last November. Anyway, it isn't a brotherhood. I joined TOSE, not a secret society."

"It takes a yes vote from all the members to join."

"How would you know that?" Rónán asked, giving his brother a surprised look. "You sound as if you have been listening in on things that are none of your business."

"Well…" How to get out of this? "Someone must have told me, Cathal or Seán maybe. I don't really remember."

Rónán's expression said he didn't believe him.

"Is that why they shortened your name?" he said hoping to change the subject.

"Dad asked if I would consider joining and I did. I am his standard bearer. My name was shortened so I am not confused with Lord Rónán."

"Did he teach you how to handle a sword?"

"No," Rónán admitted. "I do know how to use a staff well enough to defend myself. Plus, I am the only one with medical training."

What happened to my sweet little brother? Robert thought.

Rónán wasn't telling him everything. He never mentioned the new silver dagger he wore and how the hell could a staff protect him against someone with a sword?

Before the sun moved toward the western horizon, they started out, single file, each of them guiding a mule. Donal walked at the front, then came Rónán, as standard-bearer. Until they reached Cwillan the standard was furled and packed with the tent poles. Next came Robert, Fionn, and Devlin. Martin brought up the rear, leading two mules.

As the light faded to indigo, then to black, Robert said to no one in particular, "Why didn't we get horses?" He was nervous and needed to talk. Behind him Fionn tried to shush him. He glanced back at Fionn and ran into the mule ahead of him. The mule gave an angry bray and kicked at him. Even though it was his fault he said, "Damn, tell me if you're going to stop."

Donal walked back to him.

"Martin and I are listening for any sound that isn't normal here. Please be quiet."

"Who would be out here in this heat?"

"If you must know, this is the most vulnerable time to travel, at night when we could be stalked by slavers who work the edges of the Great Desert looking for victims."

"Slavers?" Robert asked. What a backward place he had come to. He wanted to say more to Donal, but he had already returned to his place at the front. He glanced up, astounded to see millions of stars. Something he never saw in Boston.

Robert was sure they had walked all night when they stopped for a rest. His knee was beginning to bother him. But he would be damned if he would ask Donal to slow down. Anyway, he had brought some medicine to ease the pain. He would have to be careful, so that no one saw what he was doing.

They didn't stop long enough to really rest. Soon they were on their feet again moving west. Sometime around dawn they stopped at a make shift corral placed around a cave with a wide opening. They unpacked the mules and placed them inside.

"I'll take the first watch," Martin said.

"There isn't anyone out here," Robert grumbled as they backtracked and moved up onto some flat boulders, then into a narrow cut in the rocks, moving upward. At the top he was amazed to find a green peaceful valley; the morning sun turned the waterfall and pool at the end into liquid gold.

"Awesome."

"Every time I see it, it amazes me," Fionn said.

"We stay here for the day and leave just after sunset," Donal said.

⌀

The sky turned from blue to mauve then to deep gold. Donal sat just inside the cave. If anyone entered the small valley they wouldn't see him keeping watch. They would soon have to load the half horses and start the last leg of their trek. For a second he thought he must have dozed off.

Martin sat down next to him.

"Should I wake everyone up?"

"Give them a few extra minutes," Donal said. "Funny, I must have fallen asleep, I thought I smelled whiskey. If not a dream, perhaps wishful thinking."

"I must have had the same dream. When I woke up I thought I smelled whiskey too."

"You're kidding?"

"Honest."

Donal turned and looked back into the dark cave. Was it a coincidence, or had someone brought whiskey with them? He remembered the puzzled look on Lonán's face as he squeezed the plastic water bottle. Before they left he would remind everyone that they could not take anything from their world that would seem out of place in this one.

CHAPTER EIGHT

Donal stopped his horse at the top of the trail leading down to the Plains of Mór, the Great Plains. Anfa, his stallion tossed his head, ready to move on. The silver bells hanging from his bridle jingled, giving off silvery notes in the clear morning air.

Vél moved his horse along side of Donal.

"You look good, a prince of the land." He turned in his saddle and glanced back at the five riders behind him. "What happened to your son?"

"He dishonored me. He dared to talk back, so I knocked him down and before he could get up I cut off his hair. So that all will know he has done something terrible, his brothers shaved him." It was the story they had agreed on to explain Robert's short hair and skimpy beard.

"Forgive me lord, he is no horseman."

Donal smiled, Vél expected his sons to handle a horse like he did. "I know."

Brid had told him six would go with him. His son, Robert, was the sixth; other than that he wasn't sure what part he played in this, should he say, adventure?

In the valley, they had been spotted up on the ridge. Men and boys gathered in groups of four and five, pointing in their direction. It was time to move on.

"Thank you, Vél."

"I will circle around and let our lord know you are here."

Donal had become a character in an epic video-film. The long hair on the sides of his head was braided with colorful leather strips, and held in place at the back with gold cord. His father's broadsword lay across his back, and the matching short sword and dagger were at his side. Both Robert and Rónán as princes of the land, wore simple bands of blue and saffron across their brows. Fionn wore a leather strip with the colors of his father's clan and Martin and Devlin wore the colors of the Clan of Guardians.

Donal turned in his saddle and said, "Time to put your game faces on!"

He urged Anfa forward.

They moved single file down the trail, once on the main road they headed for several tents on the north end of the plain, set back from the others. Vél had told him the best place to set up his tent. There were few women among the onlookers, mostly men of all ages from boyhood up. Many of the boys were probably from the village to the south. Donal neither bowed nor looked at the crowd as he rode by with his back straight, his head held high.

From the crowd that was growing by the minute, he heard, "It is a lord from the south." Another said, "I do not recognize the design on his standard." Still another asked, "Is it the four horsemen?"

Donal had to hold back a smile when he heard, "He is a lord from the east, the White Mountains, kin to Feargus."

⌒⌒

Usna heard a man to his left say it was another lord from the south. He turned away. He had seen enough of those arrogant landholders from the south. His holding on the Dubh River was in the middle, neither north nor south. Feargus had upheld Usna's claim on the land, therefore his loyalty was with the Ard Ri. Yet there were those from the south who whispered that Feargus might not be their true leader.

Words only spoken softly, and only to trusted friends, who would not repeat to the High King the traitorous dispute.

Osgar, his eldest son, tugged on his arm to stop him. "I do not recognize that standard, father."

The man standing to their right said, "It looks like one of the old ones."

Usna turned back to see what his son was talking about.

His youngest son, Osisin Og, of only ten summers cried out, "Look! Look father, his horse has bells on the bridle."

Usna studied the standard: a running white horse on a blue and saffron field. He could not believe his eyes. It was Cormac's standard that had been adopted by his only living son, Cullan. Many summers back there had been a rumor that he had died from wounds in a fight with Darlisca.

The name Cullan was on his lips. He bit back the name. Perhaps he should keep silent. A crowd was gathering around him. Usna lifted Osisin Og onto his shoulders and moved as close to the front as possible. Making sure Osgar and Pól were with him.

He bowed his head and said to his sons, "Show respect, a great warrior, a living legend is passing."

"Is he the one you remember?" Pól asked.

Usna glanced at his son and nodded.

The man standing to there right asked aloud, "Is he one of southern lords?"

"He is a lord from the east, the White Mountains. Kin to Feargus," Usna said, remembering a strange story he had heard about the mountains on the desert side.

Further down the road Roc, son of Rogan, watched the riders approach. He also recognized the standard. He turned and pushed his way through the crowd to find his father.

As Roc hurried on his way, he passed two men who glared at the riders.

"So he has come, as our lord said he would."

The other man said, "He is in for a great surprise."

"Yes, he is," his companion agreed. "Come, let us let our lord know that his plan is working."

CHAPTER NINE

Ciarán met Donal as he walked toward Feargus' tent.

"Feargus sent me to get you. It saddens me to think that it has come to this."

"Thank you for sending your son."

"It is not my place, but you needed to know what is going on."

At the end of the road they turned left. The first two tents they came to were for the brehon, the lawgivers. The larger one, close to the High King's tent, belonged to Tole, the chief brehon, who lived at the fortress of Cwillan. As they moved down the path Tole came out of his tent with several of the lesser brehon.

The lawgivers hurried to intercept Donal.

Donal sketched a bow, showing his respect for them.

"It is good to see you, Cullan Donal," said the oldest among them.

"I have come to see that the Brehon Law is upheld."

"We were told that a witness would be coming forth. Only hearing their testimony, can we interpret the law."

Tole joined his brethren and pushed his way through to address Donal.

"I will speak with Cullan Donal in private."

Unhappy, the lesser brehon moved off, some to their tent, others down the road, leaving Donal and Ciarán to speak with Tole.

Tole's hair was thinning; there were steaks of silver in it. But other than his hair Tole looked the same as the last time Donal met him.

"Feargus told me you would come. I am glad to see he was right," Tole said. "This is not a matter of law, but a matter of who Feargus' father is." He held up his hand, "Before you say anything, I know the truth, and will keep the secret, for as long as I can. Which may not be much longer. When he was younger, before he grew the beard, the likeness between you was more apparent. Now not as much."

"Are all the lawgivers with Feargus?"

"They are."

"Are you sure, that they stand with our lord?"

"They are loyal men, every one of them."

"I have seen greedy men, with less to gain than being chief brehon, betray a man they swore fealty to."

"All men wish more power. I am sure they are as loyal to Feargus as I am. Speak with your son, we will talk again later."

Donal and Ciarán paused to talk outside Feargus' tent. The sentry at the entrance waited.

Ciarán nodded and signaled the sentry, he moved forward and held back the flap so they could enter. Feargus motioned for Donal to sit down and called for ale for his guest.

Donal was surprised when a lovely young girl with long dark hair, big green eyes, and a slight build brought ale for them to drink. She couldn't be more than sixteen or seventeen summers in age. He made no comment. If his son decided to take a second wife, it was his business.

"You noticed Aingeal," Feargus said. "She is my ward, here only until I can send her to a safe place. You have not been married long enough to need a second wife. Perhaps you are looking for a wife for one of my brothers."

"You know I brought them?"

"Vél told me. So I moved to where I could watch you ride in. I see you brought my dark brother with you, as well as the youngest. Clever of you to come in from the south, so all the southern landholders would see that as kin, you support me."

"I wanted to make sure everyone knew I was here," Donal answered, as he fished the gold coin from his tunic pocket and held it out to his son.

"Keep it, perhaps one day I can return the favor," Feargus said. "Lonán tells me your land is on an island with many trees."

Before Donal could respond, they heard voices outside the tent, then the flap was drawn back and the sentry entered to speak with Feargus.

When the lords entered Donal didn't recognize either of them.

Robert took his time unloading the mule that had been assigned to him.

"How come Donal gets to go off and we have to unload everything?" he said to Martin.

"Because he is our leader. He has important things to do besides helping set up our tent. It also looks good for those watching us," Martin said in English.

Robert looked around. There were several men across the narrow road watching them. "Have you ever met Feargus?"

"No."

"So you don't know what he is like?"

"No," Martin said, as he worked. "But they say the crown rests lightly on his head."

Robert stopped, happy to have something to talk about. "What's that suppose to mean?"

"That he is a fair king, like his father before him."

"So if he is, why are we here?"

"We will find out soon enough," Martin said. "I did see him today as we rode in."

"Where?"

"He was standing along the road watching us ride in. His hair is even darker than yours. He was dressed in a leather tunic with linen leggings. He wears his hair long and pulled back with a well trimmed mustache and beard."

"If you've never met him, how do you know it was him."

"Because of the four big men standing behind him that no one in the crowd dared move closer to. Also, one of the men nodded at Devlin as we rode by."

"Interesting."

Did Martin know why they were here and didn't want to tell him? Robert thought.

Martin was the closest person to his father. His title was Guardian, but he was so much more than just a body guard. He was his father's secretary, confidant, adopted son, and gatekeeper. No one spoke to Donal without talking to Martin first.

"Moya says he is dathúil."

Robert frowned at him.

"He is considered very good looking. So good looking that there is many a maid that wouldn't mind being a second or third wife to him."

"They can do that here?"

"Yes, to insure that they have an heir, they do."

"Have you been to one of these gatherings or feis, or whatever they call it?" Robert hoped to keep Martin talking so he didn't have to work.

"Once, many summers ago. Usually it is three weeks of competitions and fun. Merchants from all over come to sell their wares. Feargus hears the petitions of his subjects, those that do not want to go all the way to the fortress of Cwillan."

"Why here?" Robert asked. "In the middle of nowhere."

"To the east of this open plain is a hill and on it is an ancient oak tree. It is called the Judgment Tree. The tree is neither north nor south, but in the middle of our land. That is why."

"I didn't see many women."

Martin didn't answer Robert, he was watching a group of six men approaching.

"Robert move back with Rón and Fionn." Martin turned to Devlin, who was helping Rónán unpack the tent poles. "Possible trouble coming our way."

Robert didn't need to be told twice. He wasn't a fighter. In fact, several times during their trip here he asked himself why he had come to this heathen place with no running water or air conditioning. What he wouldn't give to be able to take a shower.

Devlin moved up to stand next to Martin, his hand resting on the hilt of his sword.

The man in the lead sensed that Martin was in charge and stopped before him.

"I seek Cullan."

"He is with his kin."

"I am Rogan. This is my son Roc." He indicated the younger man to his right. "The others are kin. I will be happy to stand with our lord."

Robert wished he knew what they were talking about. Fionn had taught him some basic words and phrases, but he couldn't follow a conversation.

Fionn whispered to Robert, "He told Martin, that he will stand with our lord, though he didn't not say if *stand with our lord* meant Donal or Feargus."

"What can I help you with?" Rogan asked.

The next thing Robert knew the men were helping set up the tent.

"How about some help over here?" Robert asked.

Rogan stopped to stare at him, then turned to Martin.

"What happened to him?"

"He was bad."

"I hope he learned his lesson."

Martin chuckled, "Let us hope so."

Robert frowned, they were laughing at him. He turned back to his mule.

∽

Donal was surprised, on returning to their tent, that everything looked in order. His standard fluttered in the breeze next to the entrance, and their horses and half horses stood tethered on the side. He stepped inside and found Rogan giving instructions on where to place their supplies and who would sleep where.

Rogan on seeing Donal hurried over to embrace him.

Donal made the introductions.

"It is like old times, Rogan, to have you as my steward again."

"It is my honor, lord," Rogan said, bowing. "They are saying you are a lord from the east."

"Yes, and I would like to keep it that way."

"As you wish."

Donal called to Martin, "Let's take the horses over to the holding pen."

"My son, Roc, will show you the best place to leave your horses. They have the design of the Ard Ri on them, no one would dare steal them."

While they walked the horses and half horses down the narrow roadway, Donal and Martin talked quietly in English.

"Did Feargus say what the problem is?"

"I didn't learn anything new. We were interrupted before we could go over it. This isn't the best place to talk. He is in a strange mood, something besides this problem has him upset. He also has a ward with him."

"Male or female?" Martin asked.

"She is beautiful, young, and single. He is probably trying to find a husband for her."

"Perhaps we could marry off Robert?"

"Robert?"

What had come between his son and Susan Jane? Donal thought. *Perhaps his partying and drinking.*

He would never let Rob know that he knew about Susan.

"Rob never seems to find someone he cares to date more then once or twice. If there is land involved Feargus will pick someone he trusts."

"I noticed there are few women here. Do you think they are expecting trouble?"

"Less than usual. Even though violence is against the law during an ard fheis, I think there will be. Nothing serious with so many of Feargus' loyal men here. I plan to ask favors from Feargus to keep Rob and Fionn safe if there is trouble."

They continued down the road, at the end they turned toward the horse pens.

"I am to meet Feargus again tonight. After, you and I can meet and to talk in private," Donal said.

CHAPTER TEN

Donal told his sons that he was going to relieve himself. He walked north and entered the forest and turned east. At the edge of the forest he stopped. Before him was a dip in the land, where ages ago a river had crossed the plains less than a half league north of the Judgment Tree.

He stood looking at the old riverbed, now covered over with wild grass. The cut in the land was deep enough for armed men and horses to move down it unnoticed. He needed to remind Ciarán to have this area guarded during the judgments.

"Halt!" An armed sentry said as he stepped into the path.

"I was sent for by your lord," Donal said.

"Forgive me, lord," the man said, motioning for Donal to pass.

Donal climbed the embankment. Ciarán, Lord Niall, and Lord Rónán, and several other lords were waiting for him.

"He is up at the Judgment Tree," Ciarán said.

Donal nodded at the lords and passed on to the Judgment Tree. Feargus leaned against the eastern side of the huge old oak tree.

"Before we make our plan, I would speak to you on another matter. Robert, the dark one has some knowledge of the use of a bow."

Feargus turned to him. "If he is good with a bow he can compete with the archers." He sighed. "Soon the men who put doubt in the minds of my subjects will come forward."

"We both hope there will not be trouble. Only an amadan would make trouble with so many of your loyal men here. But we do need to be prepared if there is a fight. I need four men, archers and a fifth, a farrier to work with Rón."

"Perhaps a holy man from the village could help him?"

"If no farrier is here, a holy man will do," Donal said.

With the number of horses at the gathering, there were several farriers present, but perhaps not one Feargus trusted. Surely the man who cared for his horse was trustworthy. The day was waning and it was hard for Donal to make out his son's expression in the low light. Every so often Feargus would look in his direction and he would see the glint of the last light in his eyes.

"This amadan who dares to impugn my right to lead my people, went as far as to question my status as a landholder, the honor of my father and worse, they insult the virtue of my mother." Feargus paused then said, "I have sent for Tuathall. Then, we will get the straight of this and perhaps flush out a traitor."

"It is a lie what they are saying."

"Would you come forward to give witness?"

Donal hoped it would not come to that, but he would. This was Feargus' kingdom, not his. Donal wanted it to stay that way. He was happy at being a lord from the east.

"I will if it is necessary."

Feargus signaled for Ciarán, and the lords to join them. "Even so we will make our plans."

CHAPTER ELEVEN

The next day, Feargus sent one of his men to escort Robert to where the competing archers were to meet. Fionn accompanied him as interpreter. Donal wasn't surprised when he heard that Robert was better than many of the other men trying out with a bow and arrow. His son had a lot of untapped potential. He hoped someday he would grow up and tap into it.

Donal let it be known that he would be at the horse pens every morning training an unbroken horse that Lord Niall had brought with him. This way anyone who wanted to speak to him could meet him there.

In the afternoon, he wanted to watch the different competitions. Vél brought a light weight horse, his oldest son Gall would ride the horse in the last race. Niall brought a brace of wolfhounds, this would be the first year he would let his son, Kenn, handle the hounds in the warfare competition. Donal would skip the coursing, he always felt bad for the hare.

Ciarán was the first to visit him. Donal made a pretense of looking Niall's horse over while they talked.

"I would like my son, Devlin to help me with a demonstration of sword work."

Donal moved to the horse's other side. Though the animal was calm, he didn't try to lift a hoof or check the teeth.

He looked up at his friend. "With my blessing."

Two days later, while he was working with the horse, Robert and Fionn came by to watch. Donal had the horse trained to a simple head collar and single rein, in the old Irish way. He hoped to train the horse to bridle and saddle soon. When he was done, they walked back to their tent.

"What will you do with the horse when we return home? Or will you try to get the horse up the stairs?" Robert asked.

"I did that once, never again. It is Lord Niall's horse. I will give him back a well trained animal."

"I am going to be in a competition at the end of the week," Robert said. "I made the thirty archers that will compete."

"That is good news," Donal said, smiling at the pride in his son's voice.

Devlin joined Donal at the horse pens the next morning, the young man commented that he did not have the patience to train a horse.

Something else was on Devlin's mind, but until he decided to talk about it, Donal would have to wait.

CHAPTER TWELVE

Osisin, Usna's youngest son, had heard that young boys would be picked to retrieve arrows for the competing archers. He knew he was fast and hoped to find a position with one of the men. Each archer would pick one boy to help him. He had asked his father if he could go with the boys.

"Do not be disappointed if you are not picked," Usna warned him.

Osisin stood in line next to Maiú, a boy that said he was from the nearby village. Each time an archer moved down the line of boys, Osisin stood tall hoping to be chosen. But each time they passed him by, probably thinking him too small or too young.

The last archer moved down the line. It was the Dark One who had come with the kin of the High King. As he approached, Maiú stepped forward and bowed to him. Osisin made to protest, only to receive an elbow in the stomach. By the time Osisin recovered, it was over.

He watched as Maiú followed the Dark One onto the practice field.

Disappointed he returned to his father's tent.

"I see by the look on your face that you were not chosen," Usna said. "Would you like to come with me to the village?"

To Osisin it was not the same thing, but it would be an adventure to go to the village with his father.

CHAPTER THIRTEEN

On their fourth evening, Donal, his sons, and foster sons were invited to eat with Feargus in his tent.

Robert waited while the introductions were made. It gave him time to study the High King. He wasn't sure he liked Feargus. His half brother seemed soft and a bit too arrogant for his taste. Feargus had dark hair, with light eyes that were outlined by long thick lashes. Neither Robert nor his twin had long lashes, it made him think that Feargus used something on them to make them look longer and darker.

At each introduction Feargus made a comment. Like Donal, he kept his face unreadable, so you never knew what he was thinking. When a lovely young girl came forward to help the servants serve them. Robert lost all interest in his half brother and waited for an introduction.

"Aingeal, this is Rob and Rón, my kin," Feargus said. "And this is their father Cullan Donal."

Aingeal bowed to Donal and smiled at them. Robert was sure she had smiled at him longer than his brother or father.

During the meal a wooden mether cup was brought out. Aingeal filled it, while a servant held it for her. Then Fionn stood and said a blessing over the cup. Aingeal presented the cup to Feargus. He took a drink then passed it to Donal. When the cup came around to Robert, he paused, he didn't want to drink from a communal cup.

Rónán gave him an elbow in the ribs; Robert took a sip and passed it to Fionn.

The meal was meat and vegetables. It smelled wonderful. Robert hoped it was beef, but something told him it wasn't. The mether cup was passed again. Robert pretended to take a sip before he passed it on.

After the meal Aingeal brought out a small lap-harp, similar to what they called in Donal's other world a Celtic Harp, and played and sang for their guests. Her voice was sweet, with husky overtones. Even though Robert only caught one word in ten, he was falling under her spell.

Back in their tent, Robert said, "I can't believe they used a communal drinking cup."

"It is only used for special occasions. Feargus considers us all family."

"That is a stretch, Martin. We aren't all family here. You aren't, Fionn isn't."

"I give up, Robert. You are right we are not brothers, no matter what Feargus or Donal think."

Robert decided to ignore Martin and turned to Fionn and asked him how to pronounce Aingeal's name and what it meant.

"Her name is Aingeal." Fionn replied, pronouncing it ang-ell. It means angel. She is Feargus' ward, and I would be very careful if I were you."

"She is an angel, a real looker. I would love to get to know her."

Martin laughed, "That isn't going to be easy using an interpreter."

Robert frowned at Martin.

"You better take it easy," Devlin said. "If you take her lightly, Feargus might hand you your head and you will become the Dulachán."

"What the hell is a Dulachon?" Robert asked.

"Dullahaun," Fionn said, correcting Robert's pronunciation. "The headless horseman from our mythology".

Robert wasn't sure how long Devlin had lived at Forest Lake. The day he became the sixth was the first time he had met the young man. Robert didn't remember seeing him at the funeral for Jennifer Tolan. The only thing he knew about Devlin was that he was Martin's cousin and spent the day with his father, only coming back to their tent at night.

There is always a way, Robert told himself, *if you want something bad enough.* And he wanted very badly to get to know Aingeal better.

That night, Robert had a dream, not about Aingeal, but about Susan Jane. In his dream, if not in real life, he noticed the likeness of the two ladies.

Chapter Fourteen

Martin walked along side Donal down past the merchant tents. They stopped at the southern edge of the encampment.

"I don't like this," Martin said in English. "I should go with you."

"I am only going into the village to see what the talk is at the alehouse. I need you here to keep an eye on Robert." Donal studied the camp, before he said, "Keep an eye on Maiú as well. His taking to Robert is just too convenient."

"Just for the record, I still feel you shouldn't go there alone."

"I'll be fine. Vél, or one of his sons, will be there. If you can find the time, work with the archers. You know how I plan to use them. Rón is going to work with the farrier."

Donal mounted the horse he had borrowed from Rogan. He had also borrowed clothing, and wore a leather guard over his right hand to hide his ring. This way he wouldn't stand out in the village.

The small village was built at the edge of the foothills of the southern mountains. Donal left the horse at the stable, giving the young man a small coin to watch his horse; from there he walked to the alehouse.

It was strange, Donal was known by sight around Prescott where he lived, even in Chicago and Boston. But here it was different, there were no photographs of him, no public records. Rumor had it that he had died in a fight with Darlisca. His short life here had almost become a myth, with each telling more fantastic.

The small building that housed the alehouse was one long room with a few tables and benches scattered here and there, with a hearth at the end.

As Donal entered the old man behind the makeshift plank-counter looked up.

"Greetings," Donal said and placed several small coins on the counter.

The old man nodded and taking a horn cup from the shelf behind him he poured ale into it and passed it to Donal.

He took a sip from the cup, only now looking around the room. Only a few of the tables were occupied. With his back to the door he took his time with the drink.

Donal turned and glanced at the door as two men entered. The younger of the two sat down to the right of the hearth, the other approached the bar. On the counter he placed two coins, "A drink for my companion and myself."

The old man scooped up the coins and turned to the back shelf.

"Here for the Gathering?" he asked Donal.

"Yes, I hear there will be great news coming forth." Donal smiled at Vél's oldest son. The youth by the hearth was his middle son.

Vél's son took the drinks from the old man and said, "There will be much talk, but in the end what will be, will be. A blessing on you, friend." He took the drinks over to his brother and sat down.

If Donal was bumped, then there was news. But the words "A blessing on you" meant there was no news. Donal finished his drink, ordered another and listened to the talk around him.

Was he disappointed that Vél's son had no news from the talk in the village. There was a chance that he could send Rob and Fionn back to Vél's holding. He would speak to them as soon as he got back.

He rode back to their encampment along the river. The old wooden bridge less than half a league from the village was gone, replaced by a sturdy stone bridge that three men side by side could ride across. He dismounted and tied his horse to a sapling, walked up to the highest point and sat down on the bridge parapet.

The world around him was peaceful.

The Great Plains stretched out for miles to the west toward the Purple Mountain and to the east toward the foothills of the White Mountains. Overhead in a cloudless sky a flock of geese flew south, calling to each other as they flew through the afternoon sky.

A woman's voice pulled him from his reverie. Her voice came from below. Thinking he had stumbled upon a tryst, Donal stood and walked to the end of the bridge to ride on.

The voice turned angry. "Stay away from my brother."

Donal stopped, this was not a lover's tryst. What the man answered was too low to make out.

"I will tell you again, leave my brother alone. He is only a boy and does not understand your attention."

"I will do as I please," the man said.

About to step off the bridge, Donal froze. That voice; he knew that voice.

The woman cried out in pain. "No, please, no!"

"I expected your brother, but you will do."

Donal leaned over to see what was going on. There was a space under the bridge between the water's edge and the stonework. The voices were coming from there.

"Do you need help," Donal called down.

The voices stopped.

He waited.

From beneath the bridge a young woman of twenty or more summers scrambled up the embankment. An ugly bruise was purpling on her cheek, her over-gown was torn, and her hair pulled from its plaits.

"Do you need help?"

She gave a backward glance that told Donal she feared the man. Then she turned to Donal and looked him over. "It is best you ride on." With that she hurried in the direction of the village.

Donal called after her, "Ask for Rogan MacKleeta at the feis, he will tell you where I am."

The woman hurried on without a backward glance.

"I know you are there, come out!"

Lun Dubh stepped from under the bridge and smiled up at Donal. He scrambled up the embankment to stand next to Donal.

"We broke bread together," Lun Dubh said. "We are friends. Do not forget this, nor that we serve the same lord."

"Yes. But you know if she goes to a brehon, I will say what I heard going on under the bridge."

"Nothing happened, friend." With that, Lun Dubh walked up onto the bridge. He turned, nodded to Donal, and crossed over.

CHAPTER FIFTEEN

On the day of the archery competition, Donal was standing with Martin and Devlin as the young men who would compete gathered on the field. Donal was surprised that Rob wasn't among the archers.

"Have you seen Rob?"

Both Martin and Devlin shook their heads.

"I will be right back."

Donal found Rob lounging on his bed singing "Danny Boy." Fionn and Maiú sat on the ground next to him.

Donal stood over him, "Why aren't you at the competition?"

"I'm better than most of them, it wouldn't look good for an outsider to beat Feargus' airechta."

At the word airechta Maiú looked up with interested.

"That young man is not Feargus' champion," Donal said in English. "It is an insult to him if you don't show up. After all he asked to let you try out."

Reluctantly, Robert stood. "My half brother asked for me? More likely you asked him to do it."

Donal wanted to say that it wasn't true. He decided that if he told the truth another round of fighting would be the result, so he kept quiet.

"Come on, Rob."

They walked back to the practice field in silence. Robert and Fionn, with Maiú following behind, joined the archers. Donal walked over to watch with Martin and Devlin.

Ciarán came down to say that Feargus requested that Donal stand with him. The High King's personal guard moved back, giving Donal space.

Feargus welcomed him, then stood with his arms across his chest while the first archer took his turn. Neither faced the other, they talked in low voices.

"Will my brother win?" Feargus asked. He always referred to Rob and Rón as his brothers, as Rón referred to him. But to Robert, Feargus was his half brother. More like a stepbrother than blood-kin.

"Perhaps," is all Donal said. He hoped not, but it would be like Rob to win. "Which of the Lords will stand with us, which do you trust?"

Feargus named Lord Niall, Lord Rónán, Vél, and five other lords and landholders. In his mind Donal named the lords that Feargus had not mentioned. They were almost split down the middle; north and south. Donal didn't want to think of what this would mean if the problem wasn't resolved soon.

They watched the archers in silence.

After the first round Robert was among the top twenty. Then he advanced to the top ten. Feargus' best archer was good, all three of his arrows hit the target dead on.

Donal held his breath, as Rob stepped up to let fly his last three arrows. He had dyed the fletching a shade of green, white, and orange. The colors would mean nothing to his fellow archers. He checked the first arrow before letting it fly. It looked like it hit the target dead on. The judge ran forward to check and confirmed that it was on target.

Robert took his time, aimed and let the second arrow fly toward the target, it hit just left of his first arrow. He looked like he was enjoying the moment and took his time with his last arrow. It looked as if it hit almost dead on. The judge signaled that it was off target.

"My brother is smarter than he looks," Feargus commented.

"Yes," is all Donal added, but to himself he thanked the Father and Son.

"I will let him join the archers. In case there is trouble, he will be placed in the second group to keep him out of harms way." Feargus paused. "Have you considered sending my brothers back to Vél's holding?"

"The only one that would go is Rob, the rest wish to stand with us," Donal said. "Thank you, for your consideration."

"Then there is nothing I can do for your standard-bearer, for Martin, or Devlin, the son of my Guardian. But Fionn Og, I will send him to his father's care, if there is any sign of trouble. He wishes to become a holy man, when Abbot Tuathall arrives they can talk together."

"Both Niall and I will be pleased that Fionn will be out of harms way."

When it was time for Feargus to meet with the archers he turned to Donal, "Do not put yourself in harms way either."

With that, Feargus walked down to meet the archers, leaving Donal alone, to think about what this would mean to all of them. Donal had come to the conclusion that he, not Feargus, was the target of this accusation. Soon enough his son would figure this out. He worried that by coming forward he had broken one of his rules: Preserve their Celtic ways. Their Celtic Soul.

Knowing what had happened to his people in the other world; was he trying to rewrite history here?

⚬⚬

"I could have won, I am better than the king's best man. I just thought it would look better if I took second place."

Martin and Devlin shook their heads. Robert knew he was making their lives miserable and was thoroughly enjoying himself.

"Fionn?" Robert asked. "Does Maiú have family here at the gathering?"

Fionn questioned the boy. Robert watched as Maiú shook his head and caught the sad look on his face.

"He is an orphan from the village south of here."

"That is terrible. Tell him he can stay with me until we leave."

Robert's heart ached at the thankful look in the boy's eyes.

When Robert learned that they would be going into the hills to hunt with Lord Niall and Lord Rónán the next morning, he decided to take Maiú with him. He was slight for his age and could ride behind him.

"Tell him, Fionn, that I would like him to go with me on the hunt."

"Your lord," Fionn said to the boy, "Wishes for you to go with him on the hunt in the morning."

Robert was pleased with the happy look on Maiú's face.

"Where will we be going?" Maiú asked, guileless.

"What did he say, Fionn?"

"He wanted to know where we would be going."

"Donal said up in a valley, in the foothills of the mountains to the east."

Fionn told Maiú where they were going.

It was full dark when Donal started back to his tent, after talking to Lord Niall and Lord Rónán. He was looking forward to the hunt in the morning. He walked along the tents, keeping off the main road. At the well he stopped surprised to see a boy filling water bags at this hour, with only moonlight to see by.

He moved closer. "Maiú?"

The boy looked up.

"Where is your help?"

"I wanted to repay your son in thanks for his kindness."

"Let me help you," Donal said, shouldering two of the bags. Leaving only one for Maiú to carry.

Donal smiled at Maiú, his heart went out to the boy. He was looking for a home, and hoped that Rob would adopt him. Donal was sure one of his friends would take the boy, but something in the back of his head told him to be careful. That perhaps more was going on here than was apparent.

CHAPTER SIXTEEN

It was like old times for Donal, hunting with his two friends. The only difference today, were the two guards riding behind him and Rob and Maiú riding on his right side. Further to his left Lord Niall rode with his sons Kenn, who would handle the wolfhounds, Fionn, and Roc. Rón rode with Lord Rónán, Martin, and Devlin.

Donal glanced over at his son. Rob didn't look too good this morning.

"Are you going to be okay? I can send you back with Roc."

Robert didn't answer.

Donal reached over caught the reins and stopped Rob's horse. His son looked green.

One of the guards moved forward. "There is a stream not far from here, with shade. Perhaps some rest will do him good."

Donal nodded.

The second guard went to tell the others that they would catch up with them later.

At the stream they dismounted, leaving Maiú to tend the horses.

Rob followed Donal down the path to the water. The guard refused to stay with the horses, he followed them down. At the river Donal took out a clean cloth from his pocket, knelt down soaked the cloth in the stream's cold water, and handed it to his son.

"That feels good. What I really need right now is some meds."

"I have some crushed aspirin in my saddle bag."

"Aspirin?" Robert had a funny look on his face.

What was his son thinking about? Donal let it pass and said, "Moya worked one morning crushing tablets into powder."

"I guess something is better than nothing."

Donal told the guard to stay with his son. When the guard protested. He reassured him that he was just going up to his horse and would be right back.

He hurried up the path, was surprised to find the horses had been moved further away from the river. Maiú, who had been sitting in the shade of a tree, stood and came forward. He held out a water bag.

"Thank you."

"Is the Dark One going to be all right?" Maiú asked.

"I think so."

"Are you the High King's airechta?"

It was a strange question to ask. If the boy was from the village he should know who Feargus' champion was. Donal lifted the bag and took a swallow of water. It had a strange after taste to it. Perhaps Rob had made a mistake and filled the bag without boiling the water first and that is why he didn't feel well.

It was hot, Donal took another swallow of water, he wasn't worried about it not being boiled. He took a third swallow before he replaced the stopper and handed the bag back to Maiú.

"No I am only Feargus' kin. Nothing more."

From his saddlebag Donal pulled the pouch of crushed aspirin, along with a spoon. The world tilted one way, then the other. Donal tried to steady himself against Anfa, took a few deep breaths trying to clear his head; it didn't help.

Powerful hands grabbed him from behind. Donal tried to fight them off. When a rough cloth was placed over his face, his efforts became weaker. As from a distance he heard voices, then the world around him dimmed and went black.

༄

Lord Niall and Lord Rónán had moved further apart looking for the best place to start the hunt.

Rónán was surprised when, for the second time that afternoon, a guard rode up to speak to Lord Niall. This time he looked upset by what he was told. Rónán couldn't hear, but it was out of character for Lord Niall. He shouted at the man. For a second he thought Niall was going to lean over and throttle him.

Lord Niall signaled for Lord Rónán to join him.

"What is going on, Martin?" Rónán asked, as the two groups joined together.

Martin listening to his father, looked shocked. "Rón, Devlin, we have to get to the stream. Something has happened."

At the stream they found Robert sitting under a tree.

Rónán dismounted. Still puzzled, he asked Rob, what was going on.

"Tell him, Rob," Martin said.

Robert looked from Rón to Martin. He sighed, "Donal has disappeared."

Both guards had come with them to the stream, they started yelling at each other.

"What's their problem?" Robert asked.

"They are worried that this will go against them with Feargus," Martin said.

"I don't care what Feargus does to them. What happened?" Rónán asked.

"Donal went to get something out of his saddlebag. When he didn't return the tall one went to check," Devlin said. "The horses had been moved further back into the shade. All the horses were accounted for, but Donal and the boy were gone."

Martin turned to Robert and filled him in on what Devlin said. "Is that what happened?"

Robert nodded. "He went for some aspirin, and never came back." He handed Martin a measuring spoon and pouch. "They found this by Donal's horse. Who ever did this took the boy too."

"Or the boy was in on it."

"That's ridiculous," Robert said. He shook his head, "What will they do to him?"

"He is their hostage now. Who ever did this will try to get the upper hand with Feargus."

"What else aren't you telling us?" Rónán asked.

"You don't want to know." Martin said and turned when he heard sounds coming toward them through the trees. Lord Niall and Lord Rónán emerged, followed by Kenn and Fionn leading the horses and wolfhounds. As soon as they were released, the hounds lay down in the shade.

"What news?" Martin asked.

"We found tracks leading east on an old trail," Niall said. "We lost them on hard ground. We are going up into the hills to have a look. Tell Feargus we hope to return by night fall."

"I would rather be up in the hills than be the one to take this bad news back to Feargus," Lord Rónán commented.

Rónán translated for Robert.

"I don't need someone to translate for me, I caught Feargus' name and could guess what was said.

❦

It was late afternoon when they rode into the camp.

Men stopped to look at them, pointing at the riderless stallion. Robert wanted to tear the bells off the damned bridle. Every time he heard them it reminded him that there was a good chance he would never see Donal again.

Did his father have a premonition that he wouldn't return? Is that why he changed his will? No one blamed him, but Robert knew this was his fault. If he hadn't taken sick they wouldn't have stopped and Donal would still be with them.

Roc, who had left as soon as he talked to Lord Niall, stood in front of their tent with his father. Rogan stepped forward and addressed Martin.

"You are to go straight to the Ard Ri."

"What did he say?" Robert asked.

"We are to go to Feargus," Rónán translated for him.

Feargus had refused to let them sit, and for the last hour had been venting his anger on both the guards and Martin and his small party.

"How can seven men not care for one man?" Feargus asked of no one in particular. He studied Robert, before he aimed more harsh words at the two guards.

Heads hanging the guards turned and filed out.

Fionn translated for Robert.

"So he's angry, what's new."

"Oh he's angry alright. We are being placed under house arrest," Fionn added.

"He can't do that. I'm not one of his subjects," Robert said, fighting to stay calm.

"He can and he is," Martin said.

Robert stepped forward ready to protest.

In the same movement Ciarán and two of Feargus' personal guards moved forward, ready to block him if he tried to assault the High King. Common sense told

Robert to step back, his half brother probably knew how to use that sword at his side, but Robert was angry too and stood his ground. Feargus stared at him. To Robert's surprise he found Feargus was actually an inch or two taller than he was.

"Listen, if you think I plan to sit around in my tent while Donal is in trouble, you have another thought coming!" Robert turned to Fionn, "Tell him."

"Éist," Fionn said.

"Tell him."

Fionn translated for Feargus.

"So the lion's cub has teeth after all," Feargus said.

The tent flap was drawn back, a sentry stepped inside, and said something to Ciarán, who nodded. He turned and whispered something to the Ard Ri.

Feargus scowled at them, "You are not to leave the camp. Now go, before I change my mind."

Back in their tent, Robert lay down on his bed. "Well I guess I told him."

"He had something more important to do than deal with you. Tell me again why you stopped at the stream," Martin said.

"I was sick. I think I had something that didn't agree with me."

"We all eat the same food, so why are you the only one who got sick?"

Robert sat up, "I..." He studied the ground around his bed. "I ran out of my meds, so Maiú went to the village and brought me back more...I..."

"Maiú again. He has to be part of this."

"No."

"What meds?" Martin asked. "You were told not to bring anything from the other world that would look out of place."

Robert looked down. He slipped his hand under his blanket and produced a thin glass bottle. Martin yanked it from his hand. He removed the cap and took a whiff. "Fuisce! Are you crazy?"

"I buried an empty bottle at the back of the cave we stayed in.'" Robert said. "I buried another one near the..."

"Damn, Robert. What were you thinking?"

Robert shrugged.

"He wasn't thinking at all, that's the problem," Rónán said.

"Did Maiú know where we were going today?" Devlin asked.

"I told him," Fionn said.

"Great," Martin said. "All he had to do is have someone near by to help him. Wait for the right moment and they had Donal. Maiú probably doctored a water bag too."

Robert groaned and lay back.

"Feargus is no fool, he will figure out what happened. I think you better stay out of his sight."

"What did he say to me?" Robert asked, sitting up again.

"He called you the lion's cub."

"That isn't fair. I'm my own man."

"Sure you are," Martin said without conviction.

"Just hope that Lord Niall does come back tonight and is successful," Devlin added.

Robert lay back and rolled over, he didn't want to think about what had happened this afternoon. Unfortunately, the harder he tried to forget his part in his father's disappearance, the more he thought about it.

Martin dropped the bottle on the bed. Robert let it lay there. Later he planned to bury it, since the need for whiskey seemed to have left him.

CHAPTER SEVENTEEN

The next afternoon, Robert picked up his bow and arrows and told Fionn he wanted to go to the well. He wanted to get away from Rónán and Martin, he also hoped to see Aingeal there. He wished he didn't have to use Fionn as an interpreter, but that was the only way he could talk to her. He was disappointed to find that along with a servant, Devlin was with her, acting as her personal guard.

Robert watched as she gave sweets to the children. To him she was as graceful as a swan gliding on a millpond and a hundred times more beautiful, with a smile that could warm the coldest day. He was hit by a pang of guilt as if by looking at Aingeal he was being unfaithful to Susan. He reminded himself he hadn't talked to Susan in what? It was well over a year since their break up.

"She's beautiful."

"She is," Fionn said.

Robert turned and frowned at Fionn. Donal's youngest foster son was too young to think about girls.

When she looked like she was ready to leave, Robert moved forward, "Greetings. Do you remember me?"

Aingeal smiled at him.

Devlin nodded in acknowledgement, but didn't step back to let them talk. Robert frowned at him, only then did the young man move so they could talk in private.

Fionn explained what Robert had said. Aingeal talked with him, leaving Robert out of the conversation.

What do they have to talk about? Fionn's is still a child.

"It turns out she is a member of my clan, and comes from a small holding near Boweayn."

"Did she remember me?"

"She said, of course, you are the Dark One, kin to her lord."

"Dark One?"

"You are the Dark One and Rónán is the Light One."

Robert wasn't sure he liked being called the Dark One. It kind of sounded like he was being called the devil.

"It is bad enough being called a lion's cub. Who dares call me the Dark One?"

"Feargus. Everyone likes it."

"He's a real jerk."

"Speak kindly of your brother."

"Half brother."

"If you are thinking of getting serious with Aingeal, Robert. You will have to win Feargus' blessing. So you had better make peace with him."

"That isn't going to be easy. I don't like him."

"What is the problem?" Aingeal interrupted. "The Dark One looks angry."

Fionn smiled at her, "He is having trouble learning our language."

Aingeal smiled at Fionn, then at Robert. Devlin stepped forward and said something to her. Robert didn't like the way she looked at Devlin. He wished not for the first time that he wasn't stuck with Niall's youngest son to speak for him, but neither Martin nor Devlin had offered to help him. In a way he was glad that Devlin had refused.

"Ask her, Fionn, if Niall is back."

"If my father were back, I would know."

"Ask her anyway," Rob said, getting angry.

Fionn and Aingeal talked for sometime. From the expression on her face, Robert took it that they hadn't heard from Niall.

"As I said, my father has not returned," Fionn told him. "Feargus is very worried about what they will do to Donal."

Robert didn't want to hear that.

After watching Aingeal and Devlin walk back to Feargus' tent, Robert and Fionn walked out to the field to join the archers practicing. Robert hit the bulls-eye only once. One of the other archers sent his boy out to retrieve the arrows for him.

"Go raibh maith agat," Robert said in thanks to the archer and young boy. It was one of the few things he could remember.

The archer placed his hand over his heart and spoke to Robert in his native language.

"They feel your loss," Fionn told Robert as they walked back to their tent.

Robert stopped. "Donal isn't dead."

"True," Fionn agreed. "May The Father watch over him. But the chances of a hostage being returned under these circumstances are not good."

Great, Robert thought. *Just what I needed to hear.*

CHAPTER EIGHTEEN

Osisin was not sure what was going on, the camp had been in turmoil since two evenings ago. Everyone seemed upset about something that happened to a hunting party in the eastern foothills. Men were coming to speak to his father, arguing. Others were trying to cajole him to their way of thinking.

Those that went against his father's beliefs angered him.

Osisin slipped away from his brothers seeking peace. He walked down to the well. Aingeal often came down to draw water. Sometimes she gave him and the children sweets. Not seeing Aingeal, he turned and walked west towards the river. Thoughts of the beautiful maiden were forgotten when he saw Maiú sneaking among the trees.

Now what is that one up to?

He was still angry with the older boy for stealing his place as helper to the Dark One. He looked around, did not see his father or brothers, and decided to see what was going on.

Down by the river, Maiú entered a copse of trees. Osisin eased himself down among the weeds and crawled forward to a place he could watch and not be seen. Maiú sat down under an old tree. He was playing with a round shiny object. He tossed it into the air and caught it.

Sunlight glinted off a golden ring.

He was surprised when a man appeared silently out of nowhere to stand over Maiú.

"Give that to me, it belongs to my master now. Tell your kin they did well. Also that it is best not to leave any loose ends."

Maiú stared up at the man. Fear showed on his young face. His small hand held out the ring. The man leaned over and took it. Without a word he disappeared among the trees.

Osisin waited after Maiú left to make sure that the older boy did not know he had been followed. He hurried back to his father's tent. It was well past the time for his meal, he knew he would have some explaining to do.

He met his brother, Osgar, first.

"Where have you been?"

Not really understanding what he had witnessed he told Osgar that he had followed Maiú. That the older boy had met a man in the woods, and had given to him a golden ring.

Osgar laughed, accusing Osisin of making up a story to explain why he was late.

Later, Usna took the boy aside to talk.

"You must stay close to our tent, do not go wandering off on your own. There is trouble brewing. It would probably be best if we went home, but every one seems to be taking sides. I owe much to my lord and his kin."

"Yes, father."

"What is this your brother was telling me about you and the boy from the village?"

Osisin knew his father was asking about the trouble between the village boy and himself, but instead he said, "I saw him give a golden ring to a man in the woods."

His father looked at him much as his brother had.

"Make sure you heed my warning."

∽

After the two younger boys had gone to bed. Usna and Osgar sat in the tent with a single small brazier for heat and light while they talked.

"What will they do to the High King's kin?"

"Hold him for ransom. Send something to prove to Feargus they have him." Usna paused. "It is a shame, his mornings are numbered one way or the other. They will get rid of him as soon as possible. If they are caught with him, our Ard Ri will not be merciful in dealing with them."

"They would send something as proof? Like a gold ring?" Osgar asked. What his brother told him nagged at his thoughts. At first he took it as a story made up by his younger brother to explain his absence.

What had Osisin really witnessed?

"Yes, both the Ard Ri and his nearest kin wear a thick gold ring on their right hand. Let us go to sleep and see what the morrow brings."

Osgar didn't want to go to sleep.

"He disappeared in the foothills of the White Mountains. Where could you hide up there?"

"If they are smart they will hide in one of the small side canyons in the foothills until it is safe. If Lord Niall catches them they will wish they were never born."

"I wonder if that is what they did."

"What is on your mind, son?"

"What if Osisin was not making up a story? Please father, l think he may have seen something important."

CHAPTER NINETEEN

The next morning, Osgar made a trip to the well. It was the best place to hear what was going on in the camp. Nothing had changed over night in regards to the king's kin. Though it was against the law to cause trouble at an ard fheis, the men gathered at the well were talking of a raid on the southern end of the camp to see what they turned up.

Feargus had his personal guard patrolling the encampment to stop any trouble before it started.

Niall and his party rode in as Osgar was making his way back to tell his father that there was no news.

They were riding fast. It was not a good sign.

When Lord Niall and his party dismounted at the tent of the High King's kin, Osgar stepped into the shade of a tent on the other side of the road. Niall called to someone inside and a slight young man came out to talk to him. Osgar was not close enough to hear what was said, but he caught the expression on young man's face.

It was not good news.

Wanting to know more Osgar stepped across the road to speak with another young man waiting with Niall to ride on.

"Pardon, Lord, can you tell me what has happened? Is our lord's kin safe?"

Surprised, the young man said something to Lord Niall. Lord Rónán, tending the horses near by, turned to stare at Osgar. Fearing that he had spoken out of turn he stepped back, bowed, turned, and hurried back to his father's tent.

He was astonished when he found his father saddling their two horses and half horse.

"What is this? I thought we were going to stay," Osgar said.

"You kept me up half the night with your talk. I cannot get it out of my head that those evil men hid somewhere in the foothills until it was safe to move up to the mirror."

"The mirror?"

"The Lake of the Mirror, Osisin," Usna said.

"We are going up?" Osgar asked.

"We leave as soon as you are ready."

"What of Osisin, father?"

"It is best not to leave him here alone. Osisin Og can ride behind Pól on the half horse."

Osisin was overjoyed to join the party.

They were well east of the camp when Usna turned at the sound of a horse coming after them. Osgar recognized the young man he tried to talk to earlier and was afraid that this might mean trouble for them.

The rider stopped so suddenly his horse rose on his hind legs. The rider calmed his horse and addressed Osgar. "When I looked for you, I was told that you were seen going toward the White Mountains. My name is Kenn, Lord Niall's son. If you think you can help, I will show you where it happened."

Usna gave his oldest son a thoughtful look.

∽

Kenn took them first to the river where Donal was last seen, then to the trail going up into the foothills. They were halfway to the top when they found the tracks of a single rider heading down to the plains, and further on the tracks going back up. Near the top, new tracks came out of a side canyon. Several riders were going up to the lake.

Usna looked at his oldest son. "Perhaps you were right."

He mounted his horse before turning to Kenn. "The single tracks are light, probably made by a boy, these others were made by men. Do you know how to use that sword hanging at your side?"

"My father taught me well."

"We must hurry now. We have to catch them before they get to the top. Pól, you and your brother are to stay behind us, be careful, if you fall behind, I will come back for you."

"Why?" Kenn asked, as he urged his horse into a faster pace.

"Because," Usna said over his shoulder, "you can weight a body down, throw it into the loch, and no one would ever know."

Chapter Twenty

Like sentries, the trees stood at the edge of the trail, seeming to bow as Donal rode by. He tried not to look at them. The flickering torchlight made him dizzy. He wasn't sure how long he had been conscious, perhaps an hour, perhaps less. It was twilight when he woke, but full dark now. He rode slumped forward over the horse's neck as if he were still drugged. His left hand held onto the headstall. His painful right hand hung down at his side.

Stabbing pain went from his fingers up into his wrist. The pain must be what woke him. He dare not sit up to see what was wrong. He wanted his captors to believe he was still unconscious.

He closed his eyes.

They had been climbing now for some time. His guess, they were going up to Loch Airgead in the White Mountains. The terrain flattened out. They were at the top. When they stopped Donal opened his eyes, he was riding a half horse.

Maiú stood at the animal's head.

So the boy was part of this.

Behind them a commotion made Maiú stop, he held his torch up higher as he looked back to see what was going on. Donal didn't wait to find out. He dug his heels into the beast's side. In response the half horse gave an angry bray and jumped forward, breaking loose from Maiú.

Donal urged the animal into a gallop.

Surprise was on his side and when he had put enough distance between him and his captors, Donal slowed the half horse, trying to slip a leg over and jump. He found out too late that he was tied to the saddle and was dragged a few feet before the rope broke. Winded and bruised he rolled over, managed to gain his feet, and staggered into the trees. He found an old pine tree that had branches almost to the ground and crawled under it.

His right hand was swollen. It was too dark to see how bad the damage was. With caution he touched his hand, for a second he thought that his captors had cut off his ring finger. No, the damaged finger was intact, but his ring was gone.

Minutes later he heard the sound of men running down the trail heading toward the lake. Through the branches he could just see the light from their torches as they passed.

This was his chance to move on.

Donal left his hiding place and moved to the edge of the trail, from there he could see the men down by the lake. In the dark they wouldn't see him. He crossed to the other side and started moving up through the trees away from the water. It was a slow and dangerous climb in the dark.

Once he was well away from the trail he sat down against a tree to rest.

Donal woke up.

He was surprised to find that it was morning and he was still sitting under the tree. He was also groggy from whatever they had given him and very hungry. Though his stomach growled, food would have to wait for now. The fingers on his injured right hand looked like sausages and no longer bent. There was a nasty gash running from the second joint of his ring finger to the back of his hand, from there a red line was spreading up into his arm.

He didn't have to be a doctor to know he needed medical attention. The red line meant blood poisoning. He could lose his hand or worse; thoughts he didn't want to dwell on. The morning air was cold, He hardly noticed, he was starting to run a fever.

On a still morning like this, Loch Airgead looked like an oval mirror, with a perfect reflection of the rocks, trees and mountain peaks on the far side. Across the lake sheer rock walls came down to meet the water. This side had the only beach. There were only two exits to this mountain valley. Narrow passes on each side of the lake went through the mountains. He remembered an old story about another exit, it was an old trail above the upper falls.

He was heading up to the falls to find if there was a trail and where it led. His captors wouldn't expect him to go that way.

෬ා

Usna moved closer to the half horse. The animal retreated, keeping to the shallow water dragging the remains of ropes behind it. There were bloodstains on the animal's neck. He hated to have to look into the water, afraid to find the rider, afraid not to find him. The lake was crystal clear, with a greenish tint. All he saw beneath the water were colorful stones and small silver fish darting here and there.

He turned to Kenn standing on the beach. "Do you have any experience with half horses?"

Kenn stepped into the water and moved around to try to catch the animal. With slow, careful movements he crept closer, caught the bridle, and with a gentle tug he led the half horse back to the beach. He cut loose the trailing ropes and used them to tether the animal to a bush.

"Is this why we missed them?" Kenn asked.

"More than likely, they moved onto hard ground where their passing would not show, then up into one of the caves on the plains side of the mountain. They would wait until they thought it was safe, or until they received word of what to do next." Usna looked around. "Do you think he rode the animal into the water? If he knew the area, all he had to do is stay in the shallows and then go up Silver Falls to the top."

"I tried that when I came up here with my Father and his Guardian," Kenn said. "You can only get part way up the falls, then the trail ends at a shallow pool. To climb to the top you have to go back," he said, pointing back up the trail. "And cut across, climbing at an angle as you go higher."

"Is it steep?"

"Yes, very steep," Kenn said. "Too steep if he is injured."

༄

Donal stopped to rest above the lower falls. He had taken an easier trail, an old one that ran a half a league above the lower falls along the gorge to the top. He heard voices below. He leaned out, coming up the trail that led to the lower pool were two boys. He couldn't tell at this angle if one of them was Maiú.

He couldn't take the chance.

As he pulled back, his hair became tangled on a bush. When he tried to free himself the cord that held his hair back, already loose, flipped into the air. He reached out to catch it, but the cord, just beyond his reach, fell to the pool below.

He picked up his make-shift-staff, a branch he found earlier and continued the climb to the top. If the boys on the trail below him found his hair cord, he hoped they would think he had fallen into the pool and drowned. More likely, they would figure out where he had gone. He had to hurry to make the old stairs and the glade above before dark.

༄

Usna waited with Kenn on the beach, he sent Osgar to the left and Pól took Osisin Og with him to check the lower falls.

Osgar was the first back, he shook his head. "No luck, father. There is not a trace."

"Bring the boy."

Kenn brought Maiú with his hands tied behind his back. When Usna yanked off the gag, the boy cried out in pain.

"Tell me again, what happened last night," Usna said. Maiú cringed away form him. "Don't lie to me, or you will end up like the others."

"Where are they?"

"They are all dead. They refused to surrender."

Maiú stared at him and shook his head. Usna moved closer, Maiú tried to back away, but Kenn blocked his escape.

"The trail was steep," Maiú's voice was barely a whisper, "My kin told me to lead the half horse. When you came upon us the animal jumped forward out of my grasp, heading toward the loch."

"Was he well?"

"I guess. His hands were untied so he could ride easier, with only a rope around his waist. They were giving him less of the sleeping potion."

Usna turned at the sound of excited voices. Osisin Og, and Pól were running along the beach. Osisin Og was yelling to them and waving a small piece of cord in the air.

CHAPTER TWENTY-ONE

It was dark when Donal reached the top of Silver Falls. He stepped wrong and slipped, his walking stick breaking under his weight. Unable to steady himself, he fell. When he tried to rise, he slipped again and ended up on the rock shelf, the right side of his face hitting hard on the wet slab. All sound was drowned out by the roar of the rushing water, only inches from his face.

In minutes Donal was soaked to the skin.

He told himself that in a few minutes he would get up and continue to the top. In his mind he wandered back to Forest Lake. He was sitting with Moya, she was feeding their little girl. Pleasant thoughts filled his head. He was warm again. He drifted off wrapped in warm dreams of home.

Donal woke with a start.

He was freezing.

Despite the pain he clenched his jaw closed to stop his teeth from chattering. Struggling to sit up, he rolled away from the falls so he could edge his way to the trail before standing. Before he attempted the climb to the top he searched among the underbrush until he found a stout branch to use as a staff.

With the help of his staff he moved to the edge of the huge boulder. From there he could find the stairs. He turned away from the falls and walked several paces down the trail. He turned to his left, with his staff in hand he ran it along the trees until he found the break for the stairs.

What he really needed was a torch, but if he had one it might give away his position. After several false starts he found the stairs. The climb to the top was dangerous, more then once he slipped on the damp moss covered stone steps banging his already bruised knees.

Exhausted, he reached the top. He climbed under the low growing branches of an old pine tree to rest. The pungent smell of pine pitch and last year's needles, and some sort of animal scent hung in the air around him.

He would rest until morning, then continue on his way.

As soon as he closed his eyes, he was again at Forest Lake; Moya was singing to their daughter. She had a beautiful voice. As a child she would sit on his lap and sing, sometimes children's songs, as time went by her songs had more adult themes; about love and lost lovers.

He didn't want to wake up. He wanted to stay with Moya, even if it was only a dream. But wake he did. By slight degrees he was drier, but still cold. His jaw ached from the fall, as well as his shoulder and hip.

He listened.

There it was again.

Moya was singing. He lay under the tree on a dark night content to listen to her sweet voice.

As he listened, it came to him that it was not Moya's voice he heard. This one was just as beautiful, but more ethereal than hers. He sat up on his bed of pine needles and listened. The voice stopped. Now all he heard was the wind in the treetops.

Had he imagined the singing?

Minutes later, or hours, he wasn't sure, he heard the sweet voice again. Donal smiled, the soft voice spoke to some inner sense in him. He shook his head to try to clear it. The movement made his head and jaw begin to ache again.

Using his staff he pushed himself up.

Something, or someone, was out there.

He stepped from the cover of the pine branches. At first he didn't see the cottage that stood at the end of the glade, almost hidden by the trees. He half expected to see a candle in the window. Funny that he would think of that now. It was an old story Mánus had told him about the importance at one time in Ireland of putting a candle in your cottage window on Christmas Eve.

The light coming through the window was too bright for candlelight; there must be a fire on the hearth.

With the aid of his staff he hobbled toward the cottage.

The door opened, a woman stood silhouetted in the doorway, a swath of light reached toward him in the darkness. She moved back to let him enter. He hesitated. He wasn't sure how long he stood there before he stumbled inside.

He sketched a bow to the lady, too unsteady on his feet to give her a proper bow. She was beautiful, far more beautiful than any woman he had ever met.

Near the fire a boy of nine or ten summers sat on a stool. The warmth of the cottage made Donal tired, drawing what strength he had left right out of him.

No matter, Donal thought, this is a dream. I am still out in the woods, cold and wet, lying under a pine tree. For the moment he welcomed the dream.

It gave him peace.

CHAPTER TWENTY-TWO

The sun was past its zenith, Feargus and Aingeal had just finished their meal. He sent Ciarán to Niall to see if he had heard from Kenn.

Feargus glanced up, startled to find a boy standing just inside the tent entrance, unannounced. Uneasy, Feargus' hand went to the sword resting next to his bench as he studied the boy. It wasn't how he looked, for he looked like any young boy of his people.

What puzzled Feargus was how he had gotten by the sentries.

The boy did not speak, he stepped forward, and held out a pouch toward the king.

Feargus hesitated, then reached out and took the pouch. As soon as he did he boy turned and disappeared into the gloom at the back of the tent. Feargus hurried to catch him. His sleeping area was empty, with no place for someone to hide. He moved over to the other side and called to Aingeal.

Aingeal came out of her sleeping area and smiled at him. Her hair flowed around her face and down her back in a cascade of shinny dark waves. She was beautiful to look upon.

"Is there something I can help you with, lord?"

"Did a young boy come into your sleeping area?"

"No. But if you wish to check."

"Your word is enough for me. Forgive me for disturbing you."

The temptation before him was great, and he had avoided it so far. He needed to find a husband for Aingeal. He could take a second wife. He entertained that thought, before he dismissed it, and kept thoughts of his queen, Niamh, foremost in his mind.

Before returning to the front of the tent, he checked the back wall, there was no way the boy could have just walked through the tent wall, nor could he have slipped under it.

Feargus opened the pouch, inside he found two pieces of a silver tear drop shaped pendant. He fit the pieces together. On one side was an oak leaf on the other a running horse. The broken pendant belonged to his father. He carried it as a talisman.

What could this mean?

That Donal lived?

Or did he lie in the hills somewhere dead. Why else was the pendant brought to him?

CHAPTER
TWENTY-THREE

Donal woke when something warm and tingling touched his hand.

He was dreaming again, though he could not recall ever being able to feel pleasure in a dream before. He opened his eyes and tried to sit up, firm hands held him down. He smiled at the woman sitting by the bed rinsing his right hand in warm water that made his skin tingle. Around them a light floral scent filled the air.

"Is this heaven?"

She didn't answer him.

"I don't remember walking the Road of Life and Death. Or is this a dream? Of course, it is. I am still lying under a tree out in the forest."

She smiled at him and shook her head. "In the morning my son will show you the path to take. It is difficult, but your will is strong. You must believe."

Have I lost my faith, my belief in the Father and Son?
Donal closed his eyes.

An insistent barking forced Donal to open his eyes. It had been a dream after all. He was sitting under a pine tree. On the ground near him sat a squirrel, it barked again, before rising on his hind legs to stare at him.

Even though he wasn't hungry he said, "Squirrel stew would taste good right now."

Still the squirrel stared at him.

When he moved his foot the squirrel ran off into the woods.

"Cullan Donal."

Donal glanced around.

Again his named was called.

Donal was alone. The birds sang in the trees. A small grey squirrel darted across his path, stopping to peer at him before it ran on. The sun filtering down through the tree branches was bright.

The path before him was empty.

It would be so easy just to stay here and rest.

There it was again, his name, "Cullan Donal."

The voice called to him again, this time more insistent.

Donal picked up his make-shift staff and stood, heading in the direction of the voice. As he walked, the forest gave way to scattered trees. As the land became rocky the trees grew farther apart. He walked the better part of the morning and afternoon.

He grew tired, but kept walking. The trees fell away on both sides. Soon he was on a ridge, walking along the edge of a canyon on the plains side of the mountain.

It was a dangerous climb down to the canyon floor. But that was the direction he needed to go in order to join up with his sons. His staff was useless until he was on the bottom. He slid his staff down the rocks, watching as it caught near the bottom. He sat down, turned, and eased himself over the edge and started the long climb down.

He climbed down in slow cautious steps, careful of his right hand. Making sure he had a good handhold before lowering his feet and good footholds before moving his hands. He was forced to stop and to rest several times before moving again. It was late afternoon when he reached the bottom of the canyon.

Small trees and bushes to his right told him he would find water there.

After drinking, Donal sat down to rest.

When something touched his neck, Donal woke with a start, he brought up his staff to fight off man or beast. To his surprise and relief he was looking into the face of Kenn.

"Sorry, I didn't mean to startle you, lord. I..."

Kenn was checking to see if he was still alive. Donal looked beyond him at a man and three boys, then he saw Maiú sitting on a half horse. "Take care," he said. "That one lies, he is really a girl."

༄

Shouting pulled Robert out of a sound sleep. He hated to wake up, in his dream he was in Avenue Three having a thick, juicy steak and a glass of Midleton. He sat up surprised to see guards in their tent yelling at them.

"What is going on?" he asked Martin

"We are to move up to Feargus' tent."

"Why?"

"Feargus' orders. We are to stay with him until Donal is found."

"Why?"

"There was trouble last night. Fighting near the southern end of the camp. Feargus thinks it isn't safe here for us if there is more fighting."

Robert didn't like the idea of being under Feargus' care, but there wasn't much he could do about it. Then he remembered that he would be close to Aingeal. She was worth having to put up with his arrogant half brother.

He had a new problem now. Whenever he met Aingeal, Devlin was her personal guard. When his father returned would Devlin give him a full report. He didn't care what any of them told Donal, as long as he returned.

CHAPTER TWENTY-FOUR

Donal was exhausted from the trip back to the encampment on the plains. Kenn and Usna rode with him to the edge of the camp. From there Kenn would see him back to the High King. After he talked to Feargus, Donal wanted to return to his own tent and lie down. As they made their way through the camp four men came out from between the tents. The night was waning, and there was enough light to see that they were Feargus' personal guards.

On seeing Donal and Kenn, the guards hurried to intercept them.

Kenn hailed them, "Is that you, Peadar?"

"What brings you out so early, friend? Or are you coming back from the village?"

Donal leaned into Kenn, so they would think that he had too much to drink. With the hood of his cloak pulled down he wouldn't be recognized.

"Is that you Flann?" Peadar asked.

"Yes," Donal said in a hoarse whisper. He wanted to ask them what was going on, but it was taking a chance. He didn't want anyone to know that he was back until he talked with Feargus.

"Please, friend, do not tell our fathers that we were caught sneaking back into camp," Kenn said.

The other three guards laughed and moved on.

"I hope it was worth it if your fathers catch you," Peadar said, as he hurried to rejoin his companions.

From inside Feargus' tent a yellow light glowed. Devlin stood guard outside with his brother. When Lonán saw them coming, hand on the hilt of his sword, he stepped forward to see what they wanted.

"Who comes? It is far too early to see the Ard Ri."

He relaxed when he recognized Kenn.

Kenn asked, "Is your father inside?"

Lonán nodded.

"Ask Ciarán to step out here," Donal said.

Lonán moved closer, "Can it be true? Have you returned to us?"

"I need to speak with Feargus."

"Feargus will want to know you are back," Lonán said, relief in his voice.

"Tell your father someone wishes to speak to him. Please do not tell him who."

Donal and Kenn moved a few paces from the entrance and waited. Ciarán came out of the tent followed by his son.

Ciarán moved closer, "Who seeks me so early?"

"I do," Donal said. He let the hood slip back so his friend could see his face.

"My lord! Feargus will be pleased to see you."

"Do not warn him. Please, I want this kept as quiet as possible. Wait here while I speak with him," he turned to Kenn. "Go to your father, let him know that I am back, that I wish some time with my sons. Tell him that Maiú is with Usna."

Ciarán held back the tent flap for Donal to enter.

Feargus sat staring into the fire in a small brazier. Aingeal stood at his side, her hand stroking his shoulder as she listened to him reminisce.

"When I first met him, he scared me. He was so tall. I thought, *So, I do have a father*. Then I saw the look in his eyes. He was displeased with me. When he left without me to marry this great woman in a far land I knew..."

Aingeal looked up and smiled, "Lord, he is restored to us."

Feargus looked up, jumped to his feet and hurried toward Donal. They embraced; Feargus stepped back and held his father at arms length.

"My prayers to The Father and Son have been answered."

"He sent Usna, his sons, and Kenn to help me."

"Usna has a holding on the Dubh River. I will ever be in his debt."

"As will I," Donal said.

"You are tired. You need rest. Your face?"

Donal touched the side of his face, though it no longer hurt, he was sure it had turned ugly shades of purple and green. "An accident. I will go to my tent so your brothers know I am back," Donal said as he pulled his hood forward. "I will sleep there."

"You will sleep here. I had my brothers here with me, but The Dark One drove me crazy, I sent them to Lord Niall. I will send word to them in the morning."

ᯓ

Donal woke to the sound of whispering voices.

Feargus was dressing, getting ready to meet a delegation of northern lords. His voice brought back memories of Aoife when she whispered to him in the night. It wasn't that his voice sounded so much like his mothers, rather it had a quality to it that always brought back memories of her.

"Do not wake him. Let him sleep until he is ready to get up. See that he has food and drink."

"Yes, lord."

Minutes later he heard many angry voices.

"It is time we go down to the southern lords and see which one has your kin," an angry voice shouted.

Many voiced agreed with the man who had spoken. Only a few disagreed and called for patience.

"This is insanity. We do not know who took our lord's kin."

Donal smiled to himself, hearing Niall's voice.

"In the matter of my kin, he has been restored to me," Feargus said. "So, I want no more talk of raids on our brothers to the south."

It was good news all agreed.

Which of the lords was acting, which lord was disappointed that his scheme had failed?

CHAPTER TWENTY-FIVE

Rónán stopped by Feargus' tent every morning to look at Donal's hand and check the bandage.

"Who ever did this," Rónán said looking at the bandage. "They did a pretty nice job. Far better than I could have done. How does your hand feel?"

"Better. Not as much pain."

"When we get home you need to consult a specialist. You don't want that hand to stiffen up on you."

Robert and his foster sons visited him, as well as Lord Niall and Lord Rónán. Soon, he began to pace the tent like a caged animal. On the fifth morning staying with Feargus he asked a servant if he knew if Feargus had brought his ficheall board. The servant didn't know, but if he had it with him, it would be in one of his chests.

Donal went into the partitioned off part of the tent where they slept. Against the outer tent wall several carved wooden chests stood with a mat beneath them to protect the wood.

He knelt by the first chest. It looked like it held mostly clothing. He opened the second chest. More clothing, perhaps underneath the clothing he would find the game board. At the bottom of the second stack of folded tunics Donal found a wooden box. He eased it out, careful not to disturb Feargus' belongings.

Donal was surprised, instead of a game board and pieces inside the box, he found a beautiful gauze over-shift with gold and silver thread in an intricate design worked into the cloth. Beneath it, he found a saffron linen gown.

Another man might wonder about his son keeping a dress, but this dress had belonged to Aoife. Donal's fingers shook as he lifted the shift out of the box. Tears came to his eyes as he remembered the day Aoife wore it.

❦

Feargus was surprised to find his father sitting by his chest, with his mother's wedding gown across his knees.

Then the old anger came back to him.

This was an outrage.

Donal looked up, "I'm sorry. I was looking for your ficheall board."

"I do not like anyone going through my belongings." Feargus said, taking the gown out of Donal's hands.

"I am sorry."

"This is an outrage even for you."

"Feargus, I do not understand?"

"No, you never have. Have you? For all these years this is all I had. No mother, no father."

"Feargus, I..."

"You have no right."

"I will move back to my tent," Donal said as he brushed past Ciarán entering the tent.

"You heard?" Feargus said to his Guardian.

"It would be hard not to. He loves you very much. What is it that stands between you two?"

"Does he?"

"He came when you asked for his help. Even put your life, Feargus, above your brothers'."

"I had no father. I am not sure that I have one now."

"You had Niall."

"Niall, was good to me, Ciarán. But it is not the same thing."

Ciarán took the gown from his hands and carefully folded it and placed it back in the box.

"Eitne kept it for me. Perhaps she thought that Niamh would wear it on our wedding day. I never asked her to; I wanted it to remain my mother's gown."

"I remember the day Aoife wore it. She was fairer even than Aingeal. She loved him very much, and I think she had for a long time." Ciarán closed the box and set it down on top of the chest.

☙

Donal didn't walk toward his tent. For now he didn't want to speak to anyone. He wanted to let his anger at Feargus' words lose their bitterness. He remembered the words he had heard the morning of his return, at that time he had been too tired to think about them. Now they came to him unbidden.

"When I first met him, he scared me. He was so tall. I thought, 'So, I do have a father.' Then I saw the look in his eyes. He was displeased with me. When he left without me to marry this great woman in a far land I knew..."

He walked west, crossed the road and kept on walking until he came to the horse pens.

He untied Anfa from the lead line, and walked down toward the river. He sat down under a tree and let his horse drink.

Niall found him sitting under a tree while his horse grazed on the lush grass along the water's edge. He sat down next to Donal.

"I should have realized sooner that you would find a quiet place."

"Is he looking for me?"

"When I stopped at Feargus' tent, he was disturbed that you had disappeared again. He is in a strange mood."

Niall waited.

"Was something said that has wounded you?"

Donal kept silent.

"He was sure he would never see you again."

"He thought that I was dead?"

"I do not know why, but yes he did."

Donal didn't intend to get into his problems with his son. So he changed the subject. "What did you do with Maiú?"

"Her real name is Síle and those men bought her from a near relative. But then you knew that."

"I donot know how, but yes, I did."

"Usna says he is willing to take her into his household."

"Usna is a kind man," Donal said. "He was a boy when I first met him on the Dubh River."

"I remember that day," Niall said. "You gave his mother the old fortress and the lands along the Dubh River. It is still called the Butter Fortress."

"He would have been ten or eleven summers at the time."

"He has never forgotten your kindness, or that Feargus upheld his claim on the land."

"Niall, tell me, how close is Feargus to Aingeal?"

"Aingeal? Do you mean has he taken her to his bed?"

"My son, Rob, likes her, and I don't want trouble."

"Only a blind man would not notice that she is fair to look upon. And we both know that Feargus is no saint, he is a man, like you and myself." Niall smiled at him. "I do know she came uninvited when her uncle died. She cares for him. He would like to send her to stay with his queen and children. But there is a problem."

"Niamh and the children are not at Cwillan." Donal said.

"They are in a safe place only known by Feargus and the lord who took them in."

Donal figured the lord would be Niall, or perhaps Rónán.

"He must be expecting trouble there as well as here."

"No, but he wants then safe, in case there is trouble. I do not think there is anything between your son and his ward."

Donal hoped this was true. Not only did Rob like her, but Devlin also.

๏๛

In the morning, Donal, along with the brothers, Seta and Colm, were coming back from giving his horse exercise when Donal saw Feargus and his Master of Horses out in the field looking at his tall silver stallion, Tinreach. Feargus had assigned the brothers to go with Donal whenever he left his tent.

Should I go and see if I can help?

He was about to do so when Seta told him that Rob was headed in his direction.

Donal waited for his son.

"Have you seen Devlin?" Robert asked.

"No. He is probably with his father."

"We were going to go into the village today," Robert said. "Wow, that is some horse. Is that color real or do they enhance his coat with something?"

"As far as I know it is real."

"It has such a silvery iridescence to it.

"Come on, let's go find Devlin."

"Donal?"

Donal turned back to his son.

"Was Maiú really part of this?"

"Yes," Donal said. "Don't worry about, Maiú. By the way, he is a she, her name is Síle. She was sold by one of her relatives to the men that claimed later to be her kin."

"So, Feargus won't kill her."

"She has a home now."

"I am sorry for bringing her into our lives, and endangering yours."

"Rob, she only did what she was told. Come on, Devlin is probably with his father."

They didn't find Devlin.

After leaving Rob at the tent, Donal made some inquires on his own. Rogan told him that Devlin had been seen several times down by the river.

With Colm and Seta, he walked down to the river. They crossed over and sat down among the trees and tall grass, where they could watch, without being seen.

Donal wanted to see what Devlin was up to before he talked to him.

Devlin showed up on the other side of the river.

"Look the other way," Donal told the brothers.

"Why?" Colm asked.

"That way there will be nothing to report to your lord."

"We are not here to spy on you," Seta said.

"I will hold you to that." Donal put his hand up to silence any more conversation. Aingeal joined Devlin, and they sat together. Aingeal rested her head on his shoulder. They stayed together for less then an hour. Aingeal left first, Devlin followed later.

Donal turned to his two young chaperons.

"We saw nothing," Colm said guileless.

"Good."

CHAPTER
TWENTY-SIX

Followed by his shadows, Seta and Colm, Donal walked out to the Judgment Tree. He had kept busy with Rob and Rón, and training Niall's horse where he had left off. He tried to avoid running into Feargus.

Feargus sat on an ornate bench beneath the shade created by the ancient oak tree. To his left stood Ciarán and Lonán, to his right Tole, the Chief Brehon preferred to stand. The lesser brehon sat to the the right of Feargus. Sitting on the ground before the High King were lords, land owners, farmers, commoners, craftsmen, merchants and servants waiting to speak with him.

Many were here to see when the question of Feargus status would be brought up.

All men and women were equal under Brehon Law.

Before Feargus stood a merchant or landed commoner by his dress, making his petition or complaint. When he saw Donal, he stopped in mid sentence.

"Go on," Feargus said, giving Donal a slight nod.

Donal sat down in the shade behind Feargus, close enough to hear and far enough back to show that he was only an observer. Seta and Colm sat down behind him.

When the hearings for the day were over. Feargus came to stand by Donal. Seta and Colm moved back so they could talk.

"May I join you?"

"You do not need to ask."

With a graceful movement, Feargus sat down on the grass and crossed his legs. "Soon the one who insults my family will come forward."

"I never thought someone would doubt the word of Lord Niall. What have we missed here?"

"Perhaps we have missed nothing. Here comes Aingeal with my servants, will you take bia agus ól with me?"

Donal nodded.

He welcomed the chance to break bread with his son. Perhaps it would help them get past the unkind words that stood between them.

"Before I have my brothers and foster brothers join us. I must ask you to meet me under the Judgment Tree at dusk."

"I will be there."

Feargus sent a servant to ask his kin to join them.

As they ate, Feargus commented that they were in need of entertainment. He sent a servant to see if he could find Riga, the seanchaí. The servant returned with an old man helped along by a young boy.

"Lord, may I be of service?" Riga asked.

"Sit and tell us the stories of our people."

He sat down on the grass before them. The boy sat down next to him; a storyteller in training.

Riga told several stories of the heroes Fionn McCool and Cuchulian. Riga's voice was perfect for narrative, he knew where to pause, and where to go on. He launched into tales of the Four Horsemen, tales that had grown in the retelling over the years.

After telling the tale of the Northern Lord who was marched through the streets of Cwillan for his treachery, the seanchaí fell silent.

After the war with the north, none of the lords were marched through the streets of Cwillan. Perhaps they should have been. Darlisca and Artúr were gone these many years. Were any of the other lords still alive? If so, were they behind the lies being told about his son?

Donal kept silent, why ruin the story for everyone?

"Tell us the story of the fair woman of the Silver Falls," Feargus said.

Donal, who had been watching clouds over the White Mountains, looked over at his son. Feargus was watching him with interest.

"Some say she was a witch," Riga said as he looked around at his audience. "Some say an aingeal. All agreed, she was the most beautiful woman in the world. Fairer than the sun, or silvery moon, as it waxed in the night sky. Tull, a man from the far north, went up to Silver Falls.

When he looked upon her, he knew that no other woman would satisfy him.

"Tull returned many times. Each time she refused him. For it is said that she loved a tall stranger who lived in a far country to the east. Many said that the stranger was the father of the boy who lived with her. But Tull would have no other as his bride; he had to have the beautiful fair-haired woman of the falls.

"As time passed he became angry, telling her she must consent to be his bride. Again she refused him. In a fit of rage he pierced her heart with his dagger. When the boy tried to help his mother. Tull killed him as well."

Riga paused.

When he was sure everyone was listing he said, "As he looked down upon her, she turned into an old woman... Then, both mother and son vanished, as if they had never been."

Riga let this sink in before he went on.

"They say when the moon is new and the night starless," his voice barely a whisper sending shivers down the backs of the listeners, "if you go up to the glade above Silver Falls you will see the cottage and hear her singing. For witch or aingeal, she can not die."

Riga stood and bowed to the Ard Ri and his audience.

"Thank You, Riga. Please, you and your kin join us," Feargus said.

Riga did not have to be asked twice. The boy looked delighted.

❦

At dusk, Donal walked out to the Judgment Tree.

As he approached, Ciarán stopped him. Lun Dubh was already talking to Feargus. Lonán stood on the other side watching the tracker. They were close enough to see that Lun Dubh was angry, but not close enough to hear what he was saying to Feargus. The Ard Ri stood with his arms folded across his chest, his head up slightly, with his full attention on the tracker.

Whatever the problem was, from Feargus' body language he wasn't taking kindly to Lun Dubh's tirade. Donal wished Feargus would step back, he was too close to Lun Dubh, but it would show weakness on his son's part to do so.

"Is he armed?"

Ciarán didn't take his eyes off of Lun Dubh. "No."

Feargus had his sword at his side, and knew how to use it. He also had a dagger in a belt sheath under his jerkin.

Lun Dubh glanced in their direction, his face red with rage. When he saw Donal, his eyes narrowed, hatred plain on his face.

"That one does not like you."

Donal didn't comment.

Does Lun Dubh think I told Feargus what I heard and saw down by the river?

Feargus shook his head.

Lun Dubh stepped forward, fists clenched. Ciarán and Lonán moved forward. Donal was right behind them. Ciarán reached Lun Dubh first, grabbed his arm, and dragged him back.

"You are dismissed," Feargus said, in a voice that left no room for further talk.

With another hateful look at Donal, Lun Dubh pulled away from Ciarán. After retrieving his sword he headed toward the camp.

"What is his problem?" Donal asked.

Whether his son gave them a signal, Donal wasn't sure, but Ciarán and Lonán moved away to let them talk.

"He out steps himself. He asked for the hand of Aingeal."

"But…" is all Donal could get out.

"It is the land and coin he wants, not a wife. Only a cruel man would turn her over to him."

"Then you know?"

"I have heard rumors about him. Yet no one has come to me, nor a brehon, about him. It is a shame he asked for the one thing I cannot give him. I will give him time to rethink the terrible words he said to me when I refused his request."

If he didn't rethink his words, Feargus would cut him loose.

"Come walk with me," Feargus said.

Donal followed his son.

Feargus stopped under the Judgment Tree.

In about the same place he had stood the first day Donal met him here.

"I am thankful that you came."

It was the closest to an apology Donal would get from his son.

"Many seek the hand of Aingeal; including my brother. But another of good family seeks her hand. Both have the same problem, they must stay or I will refuse them."

"Devlin?"

"He was her guard when she went to the well. It is a problem I will have to think on." Feargus paused, before he went on, "You met the Lady of the Silver Falls." It was a statement, not a question.

Donal didn't answer right away. Feargus was watching him.

"I had a dream about her, nothing more."

"You met her, I know," Feargus said.

"How could you know?"

"Because I met the boy. He gave me this." From his pocket Feargus pulled what looked like Donal's pouch.

Startled, Donal took the pouch and opened it up. Inside were the two pieces of his silver pendant.

"I was sure it was a dream. I do not understand how or why. I heard her voice as if in a dream saying I had to believe."

CHAPTER
TWENTY-SEVEN

The next day, Donal looked up as Rogan entered his tent. His old friend looked worried

"There is one without, who wishes an audience. It is the tracker, Lun Dubh."

"Tell him I will be right out."

"Lord, perhaps I should get Martin?"

"He knows the law. We are all under the *Truce of the Father* at this ard fheis. He dare not cause trouble or suffer the penalty under our laws."

Donal stepped outside the tent.

Lun Dubh waited in the roadway. He had his horse and a packed half horse with him. Donal knew immediately what was going on and why Lun Dubh was here.

"Do not do this. Ask Feargus for mercy."

"And appear weak. I will go south, there are many who can use my service."

"I did not tell," Donal said.

"How else would he know."

"You do Feargus a disservice if you think that he does not have others like you in his service, or that he did not hear rumors."

"I almost like you, Cullan Donal or whatever you go by. That day at the river you were surprised, but not disgusted like many would be. He forgets I know much, even his weaknesses," Lun said, and smiled at Donal.

Without a second thought Donal's hand went to the hilt of his sword as he stepped forward, "Is that a threat against my son?" The words were out before Donal could bite them back.

Lun Dubh looked surprised, then dawning came to his eyes. "So you are father and son. No one will ever say who you are, when pressed they said you were a lord that lived on the eastern slopes of the White Mountains. The hair is what threw me off. Now I see the eyes, and features are similar."

The tracker looked beyond Donal.

Donal didn't look to see at what, you never turned your back on a man like Lun.

"Mark my words, this is not over." Lun Dubh turned and mounted his horse.

Just as the words were spoken, a breeze from the north blew down the roadway. All the standards in front of the tents fluttered to life, then went limp. A chill went up Donal's spine. With the chill came Brid's words.

"Take care, evil is in the wind, where it lands there will be trouble."

Lun Dubh kicked his horse into a gallop. Men walking in the roadway were forced to jump out of his way.

"So that is Lun Dubh."

Donal turned, Martin was standing at the side of the tent. So it was Martin that Lun Dubh was looking at.

"I hope he is wrong, but I feel we will meet again."

CHAPTER TWENTY-EIGHT

Robert was standing up to Feargus. What was stranger, Feargus spoke perfect American English. Robert pushed his brother. With the strange perception of a dream, Feargus knocked him to the ground.

"Get up again and I will fix your other leg for you."

Robert pulled a knife from his boot. Before Feargus could react, Robert jumped up and stabbed him in the stomach. Feargus fell to his knees, clutching the wound. An ugly red stain spread across his fine linen tunic; blood oozed between his fingers.

Donal woke, startled by the dream.

Was this perhaps a premonition of something in the near future. What do dreams really mean? No one could give him an answer to why bits and pieces and strange unrelated things came together to haunt one's dreams.

True, Rob didn't like Feargus. Donal could tell any time the two were together. Though it amused Feargus, Donal had made him promise that he would not hurt his brother.

When sleep didn't come, Donal decide to dress and walk down to the well. He picked up his sword and stepped outside. Colm was standing in the roadway looking north.

"Where is Seta?"

"Lord, he thought he heard something. He went to check."

To the north a scream filled the night air.

The hairs on the back of Donal's neck rose.

Without thinking he ran toward the north end of the camp. All his life he had been a runner, for exercise, for the joy of feeling alive, but this was the most important run of his life.

Adrenalin gave him speed.

He didn't wait to see if Colm was with him. The cry had been a woman in terror, there was only one woman at the north end. Aingeal.

He caught up with Seta just before he reached Feargus' tent. Two men lay dead on the ground. Donal drew his sword and moved closer to the two men standing guard.

"What happened here?"

"Evil men tried to force their way into our lord's tent," said the closest of the two men. "You must wait without, until we get word."

Something wasn't right here.

Donal had met all of Feargus' sentries. Donal put his fingers to his lips and whistled an up trill, then down again. He repeated the trill. When no answer came, he lifted his sword and said, "Step aside, or feel my wrath," as he moved toward the enemy.

Donal didn't need to look, Seta and Colm would back him up.

∽

Robert woke when he heard Martin shouting to Devlin, "Did you hear that? Get up, something has happened."

"Stay here!" Martin told Robert.

Robert sat up and rubbed the sleep from his eyes. Martin and Devlin pulled on their leggings, but didn't bother with their boots. They grabbed their swords and ran from the tent.

"I suppose it is another false alarm," Robert said to Rónán.

"Dad is gone too. I hope you are right."

Rogan came into the tent. "Hurry and dress. I will take you to a safe place."

"What is he yelling about?" Robert asked as he dressed.

Roc joined them.

"There is fighting up at the north end. We must hurry."

"Trouble of some kind," Rónán said.

Robert didn't bother to pick up his bow and arrow after he dressed. He stepped from the tent. Without thinking he hurried to catch up with Martin and Devlin.

He didn't run for long before his knee began to ache. He slowed to ease the pain. Years of easy living, too many parties, and eating at high-end restaurants slowed him further. His doctor had warmed him to get more exercise and watch his weight; it was too late now.

Behind him he heard Rónán calling for him to come back.

When he reached the north end of the camp he stopped in his tracks. There were dead bodies laying on the ground, with dark stains on them and on the grass. It was blood and worse than that; there was a head lying almost at his feet. He turned away from the horrific sight. His stomach churned and without warning the acrid taste of bile came up.

He bent over and was sick.

Rónán tried to call his brother back.

It was foolish of him to follow Martin and Devlin. Even though he had been trained to use a staff, let those that knew how to fight take care of things.

"Athair?"

Rogan pointed to the north.

The cold knowledge scared Rónán, both his father and brothers were in danger. He pulled out the standard, furled it so he could use it like a staff. He had no choice but to follow Rob.

When he reached the north end he saw his brother standing with his back to the carnage. Unknown to Rob, a man was coming up behind him, sword drawn.

Rónán rushed forward, pushed his brother out of the way and drove the point of the standard into the surprised man's chest. With a final downward thrust he let go. He picked up a sword, and called to his brother to join him.

Stepping over bodies, Rónán hated having to look, afraid that one of the dead would be his father, or foster brothers. He relaxed when he didn't recognize any of the dead men.

At the tent entrance he tried to do the up trill like Donal, failed and decided to call to let anyone inside know he was coming in.

Rónán pulled his dazed brother with him into the tent. Inside it was dark. In the dim light he made out more bodies lying on the ground. Someone knelt by the brazier in the middle of the tent. When the fire caught, he made out Ciarán. To the right Feargus stood with his arm around Aingeal. He held her tight against his chest trying to comfort her.

"Are you alright?" Ciarán asked.

"Where is my father?"

"He is chasing down the intruders, with Martin and my sons."

Lord Niall burst into the tent.

"Everything is under control, please keep everyone out," Feargus said. "And set new sentries."

"Let's go find Rogan," Rónán said to his brother.

Robert was staring at Feargus.

"It's not what you think. He's trying to comfort her."

"By putting his hands all over her. He's disgusting."

At that moment Martin and Lonán appeared from the back of the tent. Followed by Devlin pushing a captive before him. Next Donal came in, followed by Seta and Colm. As Feargus stepped forward, his right hand rose. He was holding a bloody sword. He placed the tip against the captive's chest.

The man pleaded for his life.

"He's going to kill that man right in front of us." Robert turned away and staggered out of the tent.

❧

Outside, Niall sounded like he was giving instructions on what to do with the bodies. New sentries were standing guard at the entrance. Robert looked around, men had gathered around the tent speaking to Lord Rónán. He spoke briefly to them, then placed his foot on the man who had attacked Rob and pulled out the standard embedded in his chest. After cleaning the tip on the grass, he held it out toward Robert.

"No thanks," Robert said, turning and walking back to his tent. His whole leg was aching now. Lord Rónán called something to him. He ignored it and kept walking.

Much later, he heard Martin and Devlin come back into the tent.

"You okay?" Martin asked in English.

"Did he kill that man?"

"What he does to that man is his business, not mine."

Robert sat up. "How come it doesn't make you sick?"

"I don't know, Robert. Perhaps because I was born here. Don't forget those men forced their way into Feargus' tent, they got what they deserved."

"Remember what your father has always said, 'You sleep with the devil you wake up in hell.' I agree, those men got what they deserved," Devlin said.

Rónán came in.

"Can I talk to my brother alone," Robert asked.

Martin and Devlin stepped outside.

Rónán sat down on the ground by Robert.

"You okay?"

"Yeah, I guess. Thanks for saving me."

"Anytime, Rob."

"It doesn't bother you?"

"Yes and no. I did what I had to do. Like dad did what he had to do," Rónán paused, as if gathering his thoughts before he said, "Why did you come with us?"

Robert didn't answer him at first. "To prove that I," he sighed, "that I am not lazy and just living off my father and grandfather."

"Who said you were lazy?"

"Mánus said I was." Robert waited, expecting his brother to try to tell him that it wasn't true. When Rón didn't, he knew what everyone must think of him.

"Mánus can be pretty blunt at times."

"Not like Donal at all," Robert said. "He likes Feargus better than either of us."

"No, he doesn't. Donal would have preferred that you didn't come. You volunteered. He asked if I would come and I said yes. I like my older brother."

Sure you do, Robert thought, *you think he isn't lazy like me, but I bet he is. Men like Feargus were born into a life of privilege. He'd never had to do a hard days work in his life.*

"If you can't sleep, I could have Roc get some fuisce from the village."

For just a second the thought of whiskey tempted him. Thoughts of Susan flashed in his mind. He needed to work hard to get beyond that chapter in his life. It wasn't going to be easy.

"Thanks for the offer, Rón. I'll be alright."

CHAPTER TWENTY-NINE

Martin sat with Rónán, and Robert on the grass near the back side of the hill watching Donal, who sat to their left. Donal chose to sit alone each day, listening to each petition and judgment.

"He's an arrogant bastard," Robert said, staring at Feargus' back.

"That's funny," Martin said without looking at him.

"Why?"

"Because that is why we are here."

"Because of Feargus?"

"No. Because someone claims he is just that."

"A bastard?" Robert asked.

"That he is not the rightful heir to the throne."

"It is a lie," Fionn said sitting down on the other side of Robert. "I am sure there are witnesses."

"So," Rónán said. "That means Feargus shouldn't be High King."

"We're nearing the end of the hearings, so they expect the matter to be brought up soon," Martin said.

"Does that mean that I am in line to be king?"

"No one would pick you, Robert," Devlin said, as he joined them on the grass. "You can't even speak the language. Your problem is, you don't like seeing your personality in someone else. It must be like looking into a mirror."

"That's not true," Robert said, giving Devlin an angry look.

"My father is next in line after Donal," Fionn said.

"You could fight Niall for the throne," Rónán suggested to his brother. "Or Kenn."

"No thanks."

Martin turned to look at Robert, "If you aren't careful, the two of you are going to get into a fight one of these days. I don't want to see you get hurt. You should stay away from Feargus."

"He can't be that tough, with all those powerful men taking care of him," Robert said. "I don't like the way he treats Aingeal, more like a girlfriend than a ward."

"Rob, you are so off on that one," Rónán said.

"I know what I saw in his tent that morning."

"You saw him trying to console her. She had just put a knife into a man and was on the verge of hysteria."

"It doesn't make him any less of a barbarian."

Eyes narrowed, Martin turned to frown at Robert. "I guess you consider your father, Devlin, and me barbarians."

Robert didn't answer him.

"I hope I'm not around when you and Feargus get into it. That way I won't be forced to try to save you."

Martin turned back to watch Donal.

"So what if Feargus isn't High King?" Robert said, changing the subject back to Feargus. "What is the big deal? We change our leadership every four to eight years."

"Sometimes we wish we could change them sooner," Rónán added. "Like right now, with that amadan in Washington."

"The big deal, Robert," Martin said as if he were talking to a child. "Is that it could cause a civil war, and a lot of innocent people would die if that happened."

"We are missing something here," Rónán said. "Surely they know that there are witnesses. So why make the claim?"

Robert moved away from them, lay back on the grass, and closed his eyes and said, "If you see Angel let me know."

"Perhaps it isn't Feargus that they are after," Rónán said. "What if it is Donal that they are really interested in?"

"What do you mean?" Martin asked.

"Perhaps someone wants to get Donal out into the open."

Martin looked at Devlin, saying in Irish, "Let your father know."

Devlin nodded.

Aingeal was coming with servants. Rónán reached over to wake his brother. Martin stopped him, shook his head and signaled Devlin to go.

Devlin's face lit up, he jumped to his feet and hurried to help her.

❦

Donal watched as Devlin went to help Aingeal. She would offer water and ale first to Feargus and Tole, then Ciarán and the guards. After that it would go according to rank. Today Niall and Rónán were present, so she would take care of them next.

Aingeal was in love with Feargus, anyone would have to be blind not to notice. She also cared for Devlin. Robert didn't stand a chance with her. Why did he come to that conclusion? She had land, Feargus would never let the land fall into unfriendly hands. Perhaps there were others besides Devlin interested in her.

CHAPTER THIRTY

Fionn followed Robert out to the well.

"This isn't a good idea," Fionn tried to tell him.

"If you won't go with me, I'll go alone, then."

The well was the informal meeting place for everyone to gather and talk. There were several groups of men this morning, as well as Aingeal, Feargus, and Ciarán. Devlin was acting as Aingeal's guard.

"I think we should go shoot some arrows," Fionn said.

"No, hold on. Perhaps we can get her away from Feargus."

That isn't likely, Fionn thought.

She enjoyed being in the presence of three powerful men. Fionn turned his attention to a man at the edge of the group talking to Feargus. The man was in his middle summers, with auburn hair and a close cropped bread. He worked his way around and behind the High King.

"Stay here," Fionn said to Robert.

Fionn moved closer. He wasn't surprised when a second man tried to engage Ciarán in a conversation, or more likely, tried to distract him. Normally, no one spoke to a Guardian. Feargus moved to the next group of men to talk to them. The auburn haired man moved closer.

Devlin and Aingeal moved along with Feargus.

Fionn whistled an up trill, then down, and up again.

Devlin turned in his direction.

Fionn said in English, "The man behind Feargus."

Devlin nodded to Fionn and pushed his way though the group and moved the man away from Feargus. Blocked, the man turned and disappeared among the tents. The man trying to distract Ciarán also turned and disappeared into the crowd. Fionn tried to follow him, but lost him in the confusion of a large group of men coming to talk to Feargus.

When Fionn heard shouting he ran back to see that Robert hadn't stayed back where he had been told to. The amadan had attempted to separate Aingeal from Feargus, while Devlin was dealing with the auburn haired man. Aingeal moved away from Robert. Feargus made a comment toward his brother and turned away, dismissing him.

Ciarán told Robert to move back, in very accented English.

Fionn held his breath.

Robert lost his temper and caught Ciarán by surprise when he reached past him to grab Feargus by the arm, shouting at him about Aingeal. Shocked, the crowd moved back holding its collective breath. Who would dare threaten the Ard Ri? Worse he shouted at him in a heathen language. Both Ciarán and Devlin moved in, and several guards appeared out of the crowd.

Feargus signaled them back.

Fionn moved closer. He saw one of Rogan's kin in the crowd. He hurried over.

"Please, go find Cullan Donal."

The man hesitated, reluctant to leave; he wanted to see what would happen next. With reluctance he went to find Rogan.

Robert tried to grab Feargus again, shouting all the time. Fionn was thankful that no one in the crowd spoke English. Robert brought up his fist ready to fight. Feargus watched him, fisted his hands and came up under Robert's guard and hit him twice with hard well placed punches.

Robert collapsed on the ground.

∽

Donal returning from talking with Niall was surprised when Rogan came running up to him.

"You must hurry, lord. My kin says that the Dark One has assaulted Feargus."

Seta and Colm helped Donal push his way through the crowd. Robert was held between two of Feargus' men, his head hanging down. Feargus moved closer. Donal braced himself, would he strike his brother again. Instead the Ard Ri placed his palm on his brother's forehead.

"Take him to my tent," he told the guards.

Seeing Donal on the edge of the crowd, he moved over to speak with him. "I kept my promise. He is not hurt, but it is time he learned better manners."

Ciarán moved the crowd back.

"This is not the place to talk, join me in my tent."

Donal followed Feargus back to his tent. Inside Robert was laid on a blanket placed on the ground. A servant placed a damp towel over his forehead.

Feargus stood over him, "He will recover."

Donal knelt by his son, placed his hand on his neck, and nodded. "I did not know that you had the *Power.*"

"Not much, enough to soothe my son."

"What happened?"

"Aingeal refused him, he became angry. He said some terrible things."

Donal look up at Feargus, "How would you know what he said?"

"The look on the face of my Guardian and his son told me."

Donal could only imagine at this point what Rob had said.

"When he wakes up," Feargus told his father, "take him back to your tent. When he is ready to apologize, I will think about what his punishment will be."

CHAPTER THIRTY-ONE

It rained the next two days, an all day downpour that kept everyone in their tents. The road turned into a quagmire of mud. Feargus sent word that if it did not stop raining he would open his tent to hear the rest of the petitions.

Robert was happy when he woke on the third morning to a beautiful sunny, but cool day. He ran his hand along his jaw. It was still sore. He should have known that his father would have taught Feargus more than how to play chess.

Every morning Devlin left the tent alone.

Where did Devlin go each day?

Did he meet Aingeal in private?

Today Robert's plan was to follow Devlin and see what he was up to.

Robert sat on the ground going through his things. He waited until Devlin left the tent, then got up, stretched and followed him. He had to be careful; he didn't want his father's foster son to suspect that he was being followed.

Devlin walked along the side of the muddy road until he came to the crossroad. He didn't head in the direction of his father's tent. He walked west past the horse pens to the river.

At the horse pens Robert stopped to watch a man he had met checking his horse. In order to stay unnoticed by Devlin, he moved closer to see what he was doing. The man knew that he did not speak their language, so he just smiled and nodded at him.

Just as Robert was about to go down to the river he saw Aingeal and her servant heading in that direction. He didn't have to be a detective to know what was going on.

Betrayed.

Devlin had betrayed him.

Donal noticed that Robert hardly ate anything for dinner that night. In the morning after breakfast, Fionn asked Robert if he wanted to go down to shoot a few arrows, he declined.

Before going into the village, Donal stopped to talk to him.

"Are you feeling all right?"

"I'm fine. Couldn't be better."

Donal sat down next to Robert. "Well the only other thing I can think of, is that you found out Aingeal has another suitor."

"It isn't fair he can talk to her in her own language. I feel so betrayed."

"Are your feelings for her serious, or do you want to prove something courting a girl in this land?"

"I don't know, I..."

"Rob, I don't love you less by caring for Martin or Fionn, or Feargus and Rónán for that matter. You have nothing to prove to me."

"Yes, I do," Robert was quick to come back with.

"No!"

"Yes. Grandfather just keeps me on because you asked him, or told him to."

"Your grandfather keeps you on because you have a lot of potential, and one day you will realize it."

Robert looked pleased at Donal's answer.

"Would you consider marrying her, Rob?"

"I care for her a lot. Sometimes she reminds me of someone I know."

"But would you marry her? You would have to stay here. She has land and coin. Which means Feargus would never let her go back with us."

"That isn't fair."

"You need to think about something else besides Aingeal," Donal said. "You have to apologize to your brother."

"Why?"

"You broke the law, there is no fighting allowed at an ard fheis. Besides it is the right thing to do." Donal stood. "I'm going into the village come with me."

"Thanks for the offer, but I need to think for a while.

⌀

Robert sat on the ground thinking about Devlin and his brother, Feargus. He didn't believe for a minute that his father was right, that he had been jealous all these years. How could he be jealous of Martin and Devlin? It wasn't possible he was jealous of his younger brother.

His father was right on one point. He was jealous of Feargus, who seemed in complete control of his life.

Robert waited until the end of the week before he decided to go to Feargus. Robert asked Fionn if he would go with him to talk to the High King.

"Are you crazy?" Fionn said. "He could hand you your head."

"I have to go to him. Since your father is as close to Feargus as Donal, I thought you could get me an audience with him and be my interpreter too."

"You are wrong, no one is closer to Feargus than Donal."

"This is something I have to do on my own."

After more arguing, Fionn threw up his hands, "All right, all right, I'll go with you."

Robert's plan was pretty flimsy. Yet, he knew he had to do it.

As they were leaving the tent, Rónán was just coming in with a young man, a farrier.

"Just a second, Robert," Fionn said. "I need to ask Rón something."

When Fionn joined him outside the tent, Robert asked, "What was that all about?"

"I asked to join your brother and the farrier."

Robert stopped. "What do you mean join him?"

"If there is trouble I want to help Rón with the wounded."

"Wait a second, Fionn. I thought Rogan or Roc would take us to a safe place if there is trouble? Like they offered that morning."

"Everyone is taking sides. No one is leaving until this is resolved. Rogan, Roc, and Vél and his son's are all standing with Feargus and your father."

Robert didn't know what to say. They continued down the road.

They waited at the tent entrance, while one of the sentries went inside to see if Feargus would see them. He returned and held back the flap. The interior was dim after the bright sunlight, with only a single brazier lit to give the High King light and warmth against the cool day.

Feargus was getting ready to go out to the Judgment Tree. He dismissed his servant. Only Ciarán remained.

"Do you wish for Tole to be present?" Feargus asked.

After Fionn filled him in. Robert said, "No."

"Robert, you will have to abide by his punishment."

"I know. Let's get on with this."

"Has the lion's cub come to me with his tail between his legs?" Feargus asked, standing with his legs slightly apart and his arms crossed over his chest.

Fionn told Robert what Feargus said.

His half brother wasn't going to make this easy. "I come not as a supplicant, but to offer an apology to you and your ward, Angel."

Robert thought that by putting it that way that he wasn't admitting any wrongfulness. He waited while Fionn talked with Feargus.

"Then he admits being in the wrong?" Feargus said.

When he heard the translation, Robert said, "No, but I want nothing to stand between us."

Fionn said, "Yes, lord, he understands his wrongness."

Aingeal entered the tent at that moment. Seeing that her lord was talking with Robert she turned to leave.

"Aingeal, join me," Feargus said. Aingeal moved over and stood beside her king. "He has come to offer his apology to you and to me."

"I accept," she said.

"I too. But there is the matter of punishment for breaking the rules at the feis. What would you have me do?" Feargus asked her.

Robert waited.

What would his punishment be?

CHAPTER THIRTY-TWO

Martin watched a tall slender man and his companion move to the front of the men gathered for the last of the petitions. He had been present in the morning, but now moved forward to stand directly in front of Feargus. Donal sitting to his left stood. Martin moved closer to his foster father.

Ciarán, who had been standing next to Feargus stepped forward to stop the man from getting closer. The man appealed to Tole.

"There are no weapons here," Tole said, nodding toward the sword at the man's waist. "All men stand equal before the Father, the Son, and our lord."

Tole waited.

"I see Lord Niall and Lord Rónán here. They have weapons."

"They are here as observers only."

The slender man handed his sword to a companion, who upon taking it stepped back.

"State your name," Tole said.

"My name is Siomón MacRathlan."

"What brings you here, Siomón?"

"It has been brought to my attention that the wrong man sits upon the throne of Cwillan."

Men loyal to Feargus standing among the gathered crowd aimed angry words at Siomón's back.

From the back a clear voice called out, "It is true!"

Martin turned to Robert and Rón. "You two stay out of this."

"You won't have to tell me twice," Robert said as he brushed his hand over his close-cropped hair.

Tole glanced over at Feargus, who nodded to him to continue.

"This is a serious claim."

"Yes, I wish to know who took Prince Cullan and Lady Aoife's vows and which brehon arranged the marriage contract."

"The vows and marriage contract were given during the war with the north," Tole said.

"But not by you."

"By Abbot Tuathall."

"I do not see our good abbot here," Siomón said, looking around.

"Abbot Tuathall has been sent for," Feargus said.

"That may be, yet he still has not come," Siomón said. He turned and looked at the crowd. There were only a few friendly faces there, but enough to start trouble. "Perhaps there is a reason. Perhaps as a holy man he knows he cannot lie before the Father and Son."

Martin's father said, "Insolent amadan."

"We must give our abbot, who is very busy, time to come forward," Tole said.

"How long?" someone shouted from the back.

"If he has been summoned," Siomón said, "should we wait forever? Do not forget, even if the marriage is valid, how do we know this is the son of Prince Cullan and Lady Aoife?"

"In four mornings we meet again. At that time I will listen to any who wish to speak and I will make my judgment," Tole said.

Martin relaxed.

CHAPTER THIRTY-THREE

In late afternoon, Abbot Tuathall on horseback entered the camp from the southwest. With him were three young monks and several acolytes. Donal waited with his sons at the end of the road, where he would turn to go to Feargus' tent. On seeing him standing with his sons and foster sons, Tuathall reined his horse to a stop.

Donal stepped forward, "Father," he said and bowed his head.

Tuathall placed his hand on Donal's head. "May The Father and Son keep you always, Cullan." Touching his forehead, then chest, "May he keep your sons and daughters and the children of your heart."

"May the Father keep you also, Abbot Tuathall," Donal said in response. He touched his forehead, then his chest and stepped back.

"Will you join me with our lord?"

"Meet me at the river, just before dark."

"I see nothing has changed," Tuathall said. "At dusk, as you wish."

Donal stood in the road and watched as the abbot, and his retinue rode on to speak with Feargus.

"If those three men with him are monks than I am one too," Rónán said, behind him.

"I guess they won't fool too many people," Donal agreed. "Let's go."

∽

At dusk Tuathall joined Donal at the river. Seta and Colm stayed back with a monk who had accompanied the abbot. Donal and Tuathall walked to the riverbank and sat down under a tree.

"This has always been my favorite time. Neither light nor dark."

"Mine also," Donal said. In his mind he saw Prescott's Main Street at dusk, all the shop lights seemed brighter at this time of day. Even the streetlights seemed brighter, and the colorful sky more beautiful as life slowed down at day's end. He thought of it as the golden hour.

Tuathall signaled to the monk, who came forward with a flagon and cups. The young man poured out a cup and handed it to Donal, then another for the abbot.

"Join us," Tuathall said to the young man.

The monk took out another cup and poured a small amount for himself.

"May the Father and Son keep our lord, his people and you, Cullan, in the hollow of his hand for all time."

They each lifted their cup and drank down the potent whiskey in one swallow. It was well aged and it stung the back of Donal's throat. It was as good or better than the best of modern whiskies he had tasted.

"Thank you," Tuathall said to the monk. "Give Cullan's men a cup also."

It was the signal that Tuathall wanted to speak to Donal alone.

"Ab, I will be back with the horses if you need me."

"You were glad to see me, and also, I think a little worried too," Tuathall said when his man had left them.

"I worry what will come out on the morrow. I bedded Aoife during my time of mourning, before we even talked of marriage, or gave our intent to each other."

"Not things to worry about. I will tell only what this cursed man needs to know, nothing more. So rest easy, soon this will be over and we can all return to our lives." Tuathall smiled at Donal. "We found some old books at Alibie."

"Books? I thought Darlisca's army burned all the books."

"As we worked to clear the scriptorium we discovered large slabs of stone lying against an inner wall. Your son remarked that there were several slabs like it along the inner wall. He placed his foot upon the middle one with a beautiful boss on it. 'Why is this one different?' he asked.

He called for his men, when they tried to move the stone, they found that it slid to the left revealing a hidden compartment behind it."

"Darlisca's raid was quick, they hit fast, set fires and moved on," Donal said. "So how many books were saved?"

"Only a few, and some diagrams for boats, and a recipe for uisce bheatha. There were books and vellum sheets they were going to copy. When they were attacked the illuminators barred the door, and hid them behind the slab of stone in the dry hole in the wall."

"That is good news."

"Yes. I will get a copy of the recipe for you."

"I would greatly appreciate it."

"We have been friends for a long time. Why did you choose me to be abbot?"

"It was your father's wish. As our friendship grew I knew that I had made the right choice."

"I see. What else is on your mind, Cullan?"

"Am I doing the right thing here?"

"Do you question the ways of the Father and Son?"

"No. But I do not want to change things. Anything I do will have consequences," Donal said.

"Do not worry yourself on this matter. When you help your people how can there be wrong in it?"

"I was thinking only of Feargus, Father."

"It is the same thing. By helping Feargus you help your people. My father always believed that you were the one," Tuathall said.

"And what do you think?"

"I think he was right. You always seemed more mature for your age. You brought back the *Book of Years* to us, and through your son, other important books for us to understand why we came here."

"Is he a good king?" Donal said.

"Yes. The only one better would have been you."

Donal smiled, but didn't comment.

CHAPTER THIRTY-FOUR

Abbot Tuathall moved through the crowd, leaning on his pastoral staff as his monks moved before him to clear his way. He had waited until the last petition was resolved before coming forward. He brushed past Siomón, who waited at the front of the gathered men and boys.

"Is there any who would come forward, who has information about this matter of the rightful kingship of our clan?" Tole asked the gathered crowd.

Tuathall stepped forward. "I would speak."

"Your name?"

"Tuathall MacTadc, abbot for more summers than many here have walked this land."

"What brings you here?"

"To give witness." Tuathall looked around at the crowd.

"Speak then."

"I come to set right this false claim of our lord, Feargus, not being the true heir to the throne of Cwillan."

Tuathall looked around at the crowd gathered, to see if any would try to stop him. "Before the Father and Son, Aoife vowed she had known no other man. I administered the marriage rites to Prince Cullan and his bride, the marriage was consummated that night."

"Were you also present at the birth of Feargus?" Tole asked.

"I witnessed the birth."

Donal was surprised, he had never been told.

"I was called to attend a high-born woman who was having trouble giving birth to her first child. I was stunned to find out it was Aoife, our Banríon, my lord's queen. Aoife named the boy-child Feargus Cullan Cormac," Tuathall paused. "The birth weakened her. She died in the morning. I placed Cullan's ring in a pouch that was always with the boy-prince."

"A gold ring is a gold ring. How can you prove that it is Prince Cullan's ring?" Siomón asked, stepping forward.

Tuathall turned to Feargus. "Is this the same ring that you wore on a lace around your neck until it fit your hand?"

"It is."

"Will you let Tole remove the ring?"

"No, let me do it," Siomón said. Ciarán stopped him from moving forward. Siomón shrugged, stepped back and waited.

Feargus held out his hand and Tole worked the ring off his finger.

"It looks like any other ring with an intertwined design on the outside." Siomón said taking the ring from Tole.

"One of the last two rings forged at Alibie before it was destroyed by the army from the north. One was made for our Ard Rí, Prince Cullan, and the other for Lord Niall. Inside Cullan's ring you will see his mark, a running horse and the hallmark of the artisan who created the ring. Inside Niall's ring is a running wolfhound and the same artisan hallmark. The rings created now are plain gold, with only a hallmark."

Siomón turned the ring this way and that to see what was inside and frowned. He handed it back to Tole.

"The ring proves nothing. How do we know this is the same child?" Someone shouted from the crowd.

That voice, it was Mangan's voice!

"The child was in my care until he passed his third summer. I took him to present to his father, as Aoife asked of me. I put him in the care of Lord Niall, since Cullan was not present."

This is too easy, Donal thought. Martin placed his hand around his arm and moved him over.

Tole turned to Lord Niall standing near the tree trunk. "Is this the truth, lord?"

Lord Niall stepped forward. "Before the Father and Son, I say that this is the truth. That child is here before us, and is rightly our king."

Tole turned back to the crowd. "Are you satisfied?"

Siomón bowed, "I stand corrected."

Siomón turned and moved through the crowd. There were angry words aimed at him. The crowd started to move with him back toward the camp. Lord Rónán had men in the crowd who hoped to follow Siomón and find out who his accomplices were.

＆

Only Feargus, his Guardian, Tuathall, the brothers, Donal, his sons and foster sons remained under the tree as the day waned. The voices of the crowd had faded away some time ago. Above, a slight breeze shook the oak leaves. There was a hint of rain to come in the air, the sky to the west turned silver gray.

Emotions had raged in Donal, he calmed himself, moved forward, and placed his hand on Feargus' shoulder. To his surprise his son raised his hand and placed it over his.

"This calls for fuisce," Tuathall said.

"We could all use fuisce," Feargus said, turning to smile at his friends and kin.

It was at that moment that mounted warriors charged out of the old riverbed, followed by two dozen fighting men on foot.

Donal pulled Feargus out of the way, slipped the bench back, and signaled up into the tree. From the tree five men jumped, four archers and a farrier.

The archers took up position in front of Feargus and Donal. Swords drawn, the small party prepared for battle. With a strange calmness, father and son gave orders to their men.

Martin told Rob to go over to the tree, to stay there as he took his place next to Donal.

⌒〜⌒

At Martin's order Robert moved up closer to the tree to watch from a safe place.

Seta and Colm moved from under the ancient tree branches and tried to start a fire. The fire went out as soon as they made a spark. One of the archers moved back to try to help them.

They weren't making good work of it.

Two horsemen charged the line. The line opened and closed as soon as they were through. Tuathall's well aimed staff knocked the riders from their horses. Donal hit them again and with a length of rope tied both men together. The now riderless horses plunged on, running down the archer trying to light the fire.

Rón and the farrier ran forward to the aid of the archer. Who was writhing on the ground clutching his shoulder.

The brothers still hadn't lit the fire.

As a boy Robert had taken Donal's tinderbox from the case in his office. It wasn't a box at all, only a leather pouch that held a flint and other fire starting things. He took it behind the last barn and tried to start a fire. It was harder than it looked.

"Had enough?"

He turned at his father's voice.

"It isn't as easy as it looks," Donal had said.

"No, but the books and videos make it look so easy. "

"Even I have had trouble at times. "

Donal sat down next to Robert and showed him step by step how to do it.

Clearing his head of the memory, Robert hurried to help the brothers.

"Here let me show you how."

He went through the process just as Donal had shown him, a step at a time. As soon as he had a small fire going he planned to return to the tree. When the flames were high enough, Seta pointed to the bow and arrows lying on the ground.

Robert shook his head.

Seta spoke fast, then made a movement as if he were shooting an arrow into the sky. Rón a few feet away said, "They want you to shoot the arrow."

"Me?" Then he understood. Robert stood, picked up the bow and an arrow. The tip was padded with something, he placed it close to the flame until it caught, then stepped further away from the tree, raising the bow skyward.

Seta tapped him on the shoulder and pointed the other way, toward the camp. Robert turned and let the arrow fly, as it burned it left a fire trail that would be visible for miles. Colm brought a second lit arrow. The arrow flamed up into the sky, a silent plea for help. Robert walked back, picked up the rest of the arrows with metal tips, and took the position the injured archer left open.

Feargus waited until the warriors on foot made a run at them, then gave the signal to the archers. The fight didn't last long. The horsemen and those on foot were caught between those defending the hill and riders from the camp that had seen the burning arrow.

∾

Tuathall smiled at Donal. They were standing under the Judgment Tree. Martin and his sons were waiting for him at the bottom of the hill.

"There was never a question of first or second wife. Perhaps to you, but not to your people. You had one wife, that made her first wife, your queen. Her children would be heir to the throne," Tuathall tried to reassure Donal.

"Her nurse maid left so much untold. I thought all this time she left me because I did not make her first wife. Why wasn't the child brought to me?"

"She did not want you to worry about her and the child. Nor have your son or daughter born on a battlefield. I did as she requested of me on her death bed. I was surprised when I learned that you had left Niall as your regent."

"May the Father and Son be good to her," Donal said and touched his forehead, then his chest.

"Will you be here much longer?" Tuathall asked.

"No, we leave for Cwillan soon."

"I will go with you as far as the first crossing then I will return to Alibie. We must be careful. I do not think this is over."

"Nor do I. I recognized the voice of the man shouting from the back. Unfortunately in the chaos I am sure Mangan made good his escape."

CHAPTER THIRTY-FIVE

On the afternoon they decamped they stopped for their meal on the shore of a small loch fed by a tributary of the Glas River. Devlin ate with Feargus' personal guard. Fionn, Robert, and Aingeal moved further from the main group.

Donal warned them not to go to far.

"My brother has not told me his intention with Aingeal. There is another who wishes her hand," Feargus said.

"He really likes her," Donal said.

"He will return to his home soon, what will he do then? You know I will not let her go with him. Besides, she wishes to stay here with her people."

"I have told him he will have to stay if he wishes to wed her. He has not told me his intent." Donal changed the subject. "What have you decided about Devlin?"

"I have given it much thought." Feargus turned to Ciarán. "The decision is not mine to make. The agreement is between the two of you. It is yours to make."

"I have a solution. I will speak with Devlin before we part," Donal said.

Ciarán stood up and drew his sword, in the middle of the roadway stood a dark man. Dropping their food and drinking cups, Feargus' men hurried to protect him.

"What business do you have with us?" Tole asked.

"I wish to bring a complaint before you and the High King."

Tole looked over at Feargus, who nodded.

"What is your name?"

"Some call me Dearg."

Donal didn't recognized Dearg, though there was something familiar about him. He looked similar to an old enemy.

"I want the man who murdered my father punished."

"Name your father." Tole said.

"My father's name was Taydan."

Donal looked surprised but didn't comment.

"And when did he die?"

"He died during the war with the north."

"Your father, Taydan, died many moons ago. Why have you not come forward before?" Feargus asked.

"Because, the man that killed my father is hard to catch. And I am sure will be under your protection, even when you hear what I have to say."

Dearg moved closer to Donal.

"You murdered my father. He was one of your chieftains. You killed him out of hand."

"Your father betrayed us to our northern enemy. Darlisca promised him many things, in the end things that he could not, nor had the right to give your father."

"You lie!" Dearg shouted. "You took a red-hot poker and ran him through."

Tole asked, "Is this true?"

"Yes. He came to my apartments. Tricked my Guardian into a quest to find someone that was not at hand. So he could slip into my sleeping apartment and kill me."

"This is the truth, I was there," Ciarán said.

"You lie too, as I expected."

"What would you have me do?" Feargus asked.

"Only single combat will satisfy this blood-feud."

If Feargus did not agree, Donal thought, *what other trick would Dearg spring on them.*

"I will agree to combat of honor," Feargus said.

"I do not call for first blood. I want hand to hand combat to the death."

"No," Feargus answered. "Single combat to the death has not been practiced in Cwillan since before I was born."

"But there is no law against it."

"He is right," Tole said.

"You came to my tent and threatened my ward," Feargus said. "And would have slain me if she had not given warning."

"It was not me. But the man who did this, he is in my debt. The rest I set into motion. I knew you would have to have Cullan Donal, the man who killed my father, come forward to help you. It is as I expected."

He looked around the group. "I have a little incentive to help you to agree to my request."

Martin stepped forward.

"Do not anger me more, I have men in the woods."

Dearg turned and signaled.

Out of the woods came several men, arrows notched. Another man came out of the trees dragging Fionn.

"So you see it would be to your advantage to get on with this," Dearg said. "I have your beautiful ward and your kin, the weakling who looks scared out of his wits."

Fionn's arms were bound with ropes, but he had managed to work one hand free. He caught Donal's eye and made a fist with his right hand, then held out five fingers, made a fist and held out five fingers again. He made two more fists before he held out two fingers.

Donal gave a slight nod of his head.

"Not sure?" Dearg asked. "Bring the others."

This time Aingeal was dragged from the trees, followed by a man having trouble holding Robert up. His son doubled over and was sick. Then more of Dearg's men stepped from the trees swords drawn.

Martin stepped forward, but before he could say anything, Feargus pulled his sword, "If you must, then it will be me."

"The choice is not yours," Dearg said to Martin. "Or yours," turning to Feargus. "It is Cullan Donal's choice to make and mine."

"The rules have always held," Tole said. "That Dearg can choose who fights for him, and Cullan Donal will say if he will have another stand for him."

"Decide. Or is it true, you are a coward?"

Dearg was so sure that Donal would fight, that he had never considered that he would choose Martin, or even Feargus to fight for him.

Donal stepped forward. "Name the man who will fight me."

"No," Feargus and Martin said at the same time.

"This is insanity," Rónán said. "Your hand hasn't healed yet."

"I can fight either right or left handed," Donal said in English.

From the trees stepped a tall heavy set man, the hood of his cape was pulled forward casting a shadow over his face. He drew his sword and waited.

"My new man will fight for me," Dearg said.

"Then it is settled," Tole said.

Feargus pulled Donal aside.

"Let me fight this man."

"No."

"But..."

"You once told me my problems were mine to deal with. This is no different. So I will deal with this one. Make sure you are ready to help your ward and brothers, I do not trust Dearg. He has twenty-two men in all. Watch for your chance."

Feargus scowled at him. "You use my words against me," he sighed, and stepped back.

Pulling off his cape the man said, "We meet again."

"Lun Dubh!"

"No, you are no condition to fight," Rónán said, stepping forward to block his father.

"Step aside, son."

"Please don't do this."

"I have to do this."

Rónán stepped aside.

Tole moved forward, "Do you agree to single combat to the death. Once one warrior has fallen this matter is settled." He looked at Lun Dubh, then Donal.

Both Donal and Lun Dubh nodded.

"And you, Dearg?"

"Before the Father and Son, I agree."

Robert moaned, his eyes rolled up in his head and he fell forward. The man who had dragged him from the trees, laughed, kicked at him several times to get him to stand up, then rolled him back among the tall weeds.

"The weak one has fainted." He stepped over the body onto the road and waited.

Tuathall said a blessing over Donal.

Martin brought Donal his shield and broadsword. Ciarán brought him a hand-guard. He placed linen on the back of his hand, then pulled the leather guard over it. It would give his fingers and hand protection. Donal flexed his hand a little, with the guard he would still be able to use his right hand. If the stitches pulled out he would switch hands. He pulled his sword out and was about to step forward to meet Lun Dubh.

Devlin stepped into his path. "We must talk."

They walked a few paces down the road.

"What is it son of my former Guardian?"

"I have fought this man." Devlin said. "He is strong and will try to wear you down. Watch out he likes to stun an opponent with the flat of his sword."

"This man is the reason you came with me?"

Devlin hung his head...sighed and looked up. "There is bad blood between us. I..." Devlin trailed off, as if he did not know what to say. "My brother thought it was for the best."

"I understand," Donal said. "Be ready to help your king."

Donal moved over to confront Lun Dubh.

"I told you this was not over." Lun Dubh gave him a sly smile.

Donal cleared his mind of everything, Moya, his sons, his daughter, and granddaughter. He would only think of the fight before him. When he was ready he said, "Are you going to beat me with words? Or are you going to fight?"

Angered Lun Dubh came at Donal full force. Their swords came together with the clang of metal on metal.

CHAPTER THIRTY-SIX

Donal met Lun Dubh onslaught and drove him back.

How long would he be able to hold out against him? Lun Dubh had youth on his side, and had surely practiced every day for this fight. Their fight would go on until one of them tired and made a fatal mistake.

There would be no quarter, no break, they would fight as long for as it took. The sun now at its zenith began its slow decent toward the horizon. Still they fought on, each at one time having the advantage, only to lose it;

Sweat ran into his eyes, with a quick movement Donal brushed it away.

Lun Dubh was not looking so sure of himself. Sweat beaded on his forehead and upper lip. Donal stepped back, and knew he made the fatal mistake. His right foot sunk into soft soil, or an animal hole in the grass, causing him to lose his balance. He over compensated and fell forward on his knees.

"I want to savor this moment," Lun Dubh said, moving closer. "This fight will be remembered, songs will be sung, for I have defeated one of the Four Horsemen."

"You have not won yet," Donal said, as he pushed himself up and regained his footing. He brought his shield up in time, Lun Dubh's blow almost knocking him to the ground again.

Time after time Lun Dubh tried to bring his sword under Donal's guard. Then it happened. With the flat of his sword, Lun Dubh swung hard against Donal's shoulder, sending searing pain up into his neck, and then hit him on the side of the head.

Everything went black for seconds, as sparks flew before Donal's eyes. His hand ached, as a slight giving feeling told him the stitches had pulled out. Slightly less intense was the pain in his shoulder and head. His knees gave and he was kneeling on the ground again. His sword was knocked from his hand.

Donal reached to recover it.

Lun Dubh brought his boot down hard on Donal's hand.

Donal let go of the handhold on his shield, slipped his arm out of the straps and let it drop to the ground. He made another feeble attempt at picking up his sword with his right hand, then let his weapon drop to the ground, useless.

Lun Dubh laughed. He stepped forward his sword raised ready to end the fight.

Donal only had enough strength for one more attempt and that he had to time it just right. When Lun was close enough, Donal grabbed his sword with his left hand, and brought it up. With adrenalin powered strength he thrust. Shock and surprise showed in Lun Dubh's eyes as Donal's sword found its mark.

With a groan and then a sigh, Lun Dubh tried to hit Donal again, but his movements were now sluggish and poorly timed. Donal pushed himself upright forcing Lun Dubh to stagger backward.

Blood oozed from his lips, he fell to his knees and toppled over on his face. The ground around him soaked up his blood as life left him.

Tuathall stepped forward, knelt by the fallen warrior and declared him dead. Before standing he gave Lun Dubh his last rites and touched his forehead, then his chest.

"This is settled now," Tole said. "You agreed to hand to hand combat. You will leave Cullan Donal and all his kin in peace."

Dearg bowed to Tole and Feargus.

"Before I go, I have something that belongs to you," Dearg said fishing a gold ring out of his pocket.

He stepped forward as if to give it to Donal. At the last second he tossed the ring into the air. Donal reached forward to catch it, at the same time Dearg's dagger blade caught the sunlight.

"It is too bad my men did not kill you when they caught you up in the hills," Dearg said, as he aimed his dagger at Donal's throat. Before his dagger found its mark, his eyes went wide with surprise. He gave a stran-gled gasp and staggered forward.

Unsteady himself, Donal stepped aside and let him fall to the ground. He stared at the two tricolored arrows placed side by side in Dearg's back.

Robert stepped from the trees on the far side of the road. He had another arrow notched, and the rest of his arrows placed in the crook of a young tree, ready to take on any man who tried to stop him.

Donal glanced down at his hand, blood was flowing freely now, soaking the ground. Weak from loss of blood Donal stepped away from Dearg and sank to his knees.

The world around Donal passed away, soon he would grow cold.

Chapter Thirty-Seven

His body flush with life, Donal ran up the road toward the fortress of Cwillan. Niall ran ahead of him. His friend turned and chided him to run faster. Siobhán stepped into his path, Donal dodged around her. After the war was over she would become Niall's bride.

Donal had won that day.

He stopped, and watched as Niall moved on into the distance, only a memory somewhere in his mind. The sound of the cheering crowd dimmed as the cold caught him, his life force drained out of his body, and he let go.

From a long distance he heard fighting, shouts, cries of the wounded. Feargus was calling for his horse, and Tuathall, his old friend, was saying a prayer.

The sounds resolved into silence.

Donal walked on a wind swept road that snaked off into the distance. He moved down the road, nothing mattered now. All he had to do is follow the road to its end.

Something warm was placed on his forehead. For a heartbeat he seemed suspended, not part of either world.

Donal was almost, but not quiet conscious when Feargus shouted, "No!"

"There is no hope. Let me give him his last rites."

"No!"

Then Rónán cried, "Help me, we need to move him into the sun. He's going into shock. I need some cloth for bandages and a blanket. Fuisce, does anyone have fuisce?"

"Let me go," Donal said.

"I cannot," Feargus said, calm now.

"Why, Feargus?"

"We have to talk."

"There were better times to talk."

"Yes, and now it is almost too late."

"You cannot change what will be," Donal said.

"I would have stood for you, but you used my words against me."

Donal couldn't see his son, but he knew he was there by his side. Donal shivered, even though his arm felt as if it was on fire.

From the other world he heard, "He's growing cold again. We need more blankets."

"No! Bring my cloak the one with the fur lining."

Something soft and warm was tucked around Donal.

In the blink of any eye he was standing under the Judgment Tree.

"Why here?"

"To keep you from going to the other place."

Donal started to turn around, but stopped, his son would have trouble holding the illusion of a moving image.

"Don't do this. It is very dangerous, Feargus."

"I must do this." His son's voice was soft, but firm.

"If I am to go to the Father and Son, you cannot stop me."

"You left me to go to their mother," Feargus said.

Was he jealous of his brothers?

"I did not abandon you."

"Later, I knew that you had done what you thought was for the best for me. You came when I became a Son of Déaglán, and again when I became Ard Ri of our people. And on the day I married Niamh."

"You knew, when you became a Son of Déaglán?"

"Only one servant sits in the chapel, and that night there were two." Feargus paused. "When I saw my brothers the old anger came back. You left me for them."

"I never stopped loving you. I am so sorry. I..." Donal groaned, the pain in his hand became intense, were they going to cut it off?

"Do not speak. Please. Save your strength. Let me talk. I know in my head the truth, but my heart told me a different story."

Strange, Donal thought, *Rob is jealous of you, and you of him.*

His vision grew dim.

"Do not leave me, father!"

In reality the choice was not his, nor Feargus' to make.

I lámha an Athar. It was in the hands of the Father.

The last thing Donal heard was a familiar voice saying he had to believe.

For a long time Donal didn't realize that his eyes were open. He was staring up at the sky; it was a starless night. Around him the torchlight flickered casting strange shadows on the trees. In the distance came the thunder of horses on the road.

Robert sat down next to Rónán. He was fascinated at what Feargus was doing, he had his left hand on his father's forehead and with his right hand he had a firm grip on Donal's left hand. He was talking, or perhaps praying. The words were so low Robert couldn't make them out.

Trying to shift into a better position, Robert groaned. In the morning he would be stiff from the kicks, but he needed to pretend to faint. Funny, he had had no plan, still it had worked. He stopped Dearg from killing his father. His father. When was the last time he called Donal father and meant it?

Robert watched while a fur-lined cloak was tucked around Donal. The sun went down, torches were lit. In a group to their left sat the fourteen men captured in the woods. The warriors seeing their leader and his champion dead, had turned and ran. Those that refused to surrender died. Their bodies lay in a row along with Lun Dubh and Dearg closer to the trees, with several of Feargus' fallen men.

Still Feargus went on and on, until he became hoarse.

"I thought there for a moment that Feargus was going to strike Tuathall," Robert said.

"Me too."

"What is he doing?"

"I think, he is holding him here, with us. Until Niall gets here. I am glad I can't hear what he is saying."

"Why?" Robert would love to know what Feargus was saying.

"I think, Robert, that it is something personal between the two of them."

"I guess he isn't so bad. He would have taken Donal's place."

"So would have Martin, but Donal refused."

"He's awake, his eyes are open." Robert shouted, then stopped and listened. "I hear horses!"

CHAPTER
THIRTY-EIGHT

"Da. Da!"

Donal opened his eyes at Rón's insistent voice.

"We are going to lift you, place you on a support before we put you in the wagon."

"Get my horse, I can ride."

"I can't let you do that, you've lost a lot of blood."

"Get my horse," Donal said, and coughed. "Water."

Rónán helped him sit up a little, while he held a cup for Donal to drink from. He became dizzy. When his son eased him back down, he closed his eyes again. *In a minute I will get up*, he thought, as he drifted back to sleep.

When he woke up again later, the slow steady creak of wood told him that he was in a wagon. Its rhythmic movement lulled him back to sleep.

When Donal woke again, he wasn't sure if it was days or just hours later. His pallet was lifted by four men. Martin and Devlin were facing him, they looked grim as they carried him up an incline or perhaps stairs. They looked like pall-bearers to Donal. He wanted to speak to them, tell them he was all right, but his tongue was dry and too thick in his mouth to form words.

In a few minutes he drifted off again.

～

Martin found Rón down in the stable, sitting on a stool he had pushed back against the wall. He almost missed the younger man sitting in the dark corner. He placed the torch in a holder. Rón looked tired from sitting up most of the night with his father.

It was easier for Martin to sit down on the ground next to him, than trying to balance on a three-legged stool.

"You need to let Fionn or me take over for you at night."

"I know," Rónán said, as he brushed his fingers first under his right eye, then his left. "I just think each night, that this will be the night he wakes up."

"Neither Lord Niall nor Feargus seem worried. He needs his rest."

"I know, but it has been weeks now and he still is never awake for more then a few minutes at most. He doesn't speak or respond when we talk to him. He is the thinnest I have ever seen him."

"When he wakes up and starts eating solid food, he will put back on the weight he has lost, and have plenty to say to all of us."

"I can't get it out of my head that I should have taken him home, I was so sure that I was right, that I let his friends talk us into coming here to Faolán. At home we would have better doctors."

"He has the best doctor he could have."

Rón looked up puzzled.

"He has you, what better doctor could he have?" Martin asked. "You know the trek through the desert would have been too much for him."

Rón ran his hand through his long hair, leaned back and closed his eyes. When he opened them again he said, "I hope you are right."

CHAPTER THIRTY-NINE

Out of the fog of deep sleep Donal drifted into wakefulness. It was the voices that actually woke him, he recognized them and opened his eyes.

"The house should go to the oldest," Robert said. "Isn't that what the lawgivers would agree to?"

With difficulty Donal turned his head so he had a better view of the room. Rob sat in front of the hearth, where a fire roared. From time to time Rob rubbed his arms, as if he was cold. Martin was standing across from him by the wall.

Rónán sat down on the chair by the bed. "Shut up, Robert."

"He is right, Rón," Martin said.

The seat creaked from his weight as Rónán turned, Donal couldn't see his expression.

"Don't looked so surprised, Rón. It is true under Brehon Law the oldest gets the house."

"I am surprised you are backing me up, Martin," Robert said.

Rónán shook his head. "I can't believe you two."

"He is right," Fionn said from the bed on the other side of the hearth. "It goes to the oldest."

"That means you are still out Robert. It goes to Feargus as oldest," Martin said.

"What would he do with it?"

"He would give it to Moya. Anyway it is not going to come to that."

Even though they were speaking in English, Donal didn't understand what they were talking about. He closed his eyes. He was tired and just wanted to sleep.

෪

When Donal opened his eyes the room was empty, accept for Rónán, who still sat by the bed. His head was bent and he seemed to be muttering to himself. At least that is what Donal thought until his son raised his head and touched his forehead, then his chest.

"Did Fionn convert you?" His voice sounded weak, as well as hoarse and scratchy to his ears.

Rón's mouth dropped open and his eyes grew large with surprise. "Say that again."

Donal repeated his question, his voice a whisper.

Rónán jumped up, the chair fell over with a clatter. He didn't stop to right it. He hurried to the door, opened it, and spoke to someone in the hall.

He came back to the bed, picked up the chair and sat down. "Welcome back, Da."

Lord Rónán hurried into the room, behind him were Martin, Robert, Fionn and the brothers.

"Please, someone send for Mór," Lord Rónán said. "There are too many here, please wait in the hall until my wife has seen Cullan Donal."

Rón stood to let his name sake take the chair. Instead, the Lord of Faolán, knelt by the bed and took Donal's left hand in his. "It is pleased I am that you are awake."

Mór came into the room, closed the door and stood with her back to it.

"I am at Faolán," it was a statement not a question. "I do not remember coming here.'

Mór stepped forward and put her hand on her husband's shoulder. "Let me speak with him."

Lord Rónán stood. "We will talk later."

"Rón, please wait in the hall," Mór said.

When they were alone, she placed her hand on Donal's forehead and smiled. "You are thinner, but soon you will be well. It is good to have you back."

Donal's face was warm and itchy. When he tried to scratch his face he was puzzled when his right arm didn't move. With his left hand he pulled back the blanket and was amazed to see that his right arm was in a sling and tied to a belt around his waist.

He pulled the cover back up. He wore nothing but the briefest of underclothes.

"Do you remember why you came to Cwillan?" Mór asked softly, as if the question had no importance.

He was forced to think for a minute, before he answered. "Yes, to help Feargus. We stood together at the Judgment Tree and then...there was a fight and..." Donal watched Mór, she was the sister of his former Guardian, Ciarán.

Mór smiled at him. "It is good to hear that you remember. This was the closest fortress to take you to after the fight. I will let the one who is a healer see you now."

Outside in the hall Mór spoke to someone, probably Rón, in hushed tones.

☙

"Feargus gave me Lightning, told me the route to take to catch up with Niall," Martin said. "Can you believe that? No one rides his horse, not even his groom."

Donal tried to smile, but it hurt, his lips were dry and chapped.

"I met Niall in a hurry to get back to you. He knew something was wrong. I barely told him what had happened when he urged his horse back to you."

In his mind Donal saw Niall yelling to his horse to run faster. Niall was his aman chara, his soul mate, his mentor.

"He made it."

"Yes and no," Martin said, as he shook his head.

"But," Donal said raising his hands, realizing too late that his right hand was bandaged several inches above his wrist with a piece of wood beneath to immobilize it and his arm was still in a sling.

"Feargus, held you here."

Donal tried to get up, which wasn't easy with his right arm in a sling. Martin reached over to stop him.

"Martin, I need to get up."

Martin shook his head.

"You don't understand, I need to get up."

"Oh, yes. I'll get Seta to help."

Back in bed Donal asked Martin to get him some food and a little ale. Seta came in to sit by the bed.

"It is good that you will be well soon."

"Have the leaves started to turn yet?" Donal asked the young man.

"They have turned…" Seta stopped.

"What month is it, Seta?"

"Late Meán Fómhair."

"September."

He had been ill for over a month.

გებ

Donal sat up in bed, playing chess with Rob. He studied the board. If he played his A game, it would be over too soon. He chose to make a minor mistake that wouldn't cost him the game, but would allow them to play longer.

"Martin and Fionn, even Seta and his brother go to the stable everyday. They seem to love their horses more then anything else in the word."

Cormac's words came back to Donal. "My father told me once to be good to my horse. I asked why. And he said, "The horses saved us. Remember that always.""

"What is that suppose to mean?"

"I don't know, Rob, but Niall said that he had also heard it from his grandfather."

Donal was toying with the idea of sending Martin and Fionn back to get word to Moya. He decided it was too dangerous this time of year. It was a minor comment by Rob that helped him make up his mind.

His son was just making small talk.

"Did you know that Mánus came to talk to me?"

"Yes, he told me," Donal said as he studied the chessboard.

Robert made his move. "Is Alvin O'Brien like Martin?"

"Do you mean is he a Guardian? No." Donal took his time making his move.

"Funny, I saw him that day, right after I spoke with Mánus. I figured they were together." Robert made his move. "I was waiting to pay my bill at Avenue Three. I saw him through the window."

"Perhaps he was in town with Mánus," Donal said. His tone was calm, inside he was anything but calm. Was Alvin after Mánus? Was he stalking him? He remembered the profiler's words, that the letter writer would act on his threats. The thought scared Donal. He would have to send Martin and Fionn back after all to warn Mánus.

He would talk to Martin as soon as possible.

CHAPTER FORTY

Mór was coming back from the village along the lake path with one of the serving girls.

The girl stopped and pointed, "Look, the Wild Man."

Mór looked in the direction the girl indicated and was surprised to see Cullan Donal, who his sons and foster sons simply called Donal; and her son, Martin. They were down at the water's edge, in the area where they launched the boats.

The night sentries were the first to mention seeing him. At first he came out in the courtyard, only after half a moon did he try the stairs. The sentry on duty seeing that he was having difficulty stepped forward to help him. Cullan Donal motioned him back. Soon he was walking the curtain wall and going to the stable to care for his horse in the dead of night.

It was good that he had finally come out of his room during sunlight. He was far too pale.

She could have taken a stick to Seta for letting him know how much time had passed since his fight with

Lun Dubh. Her husband cautioned her not to, the young man would become the leader of the Youths in the spring. Cullan Donal was Seta's and his brother's sponsor. "If he was not displeased with Seta, then we should remain silent."

"Go on to the kitchen," Mór said, handing the girl her burlap satchel.

It annoyed Mór that the servants, and even her own daughters called him the Wild Man because of his long hair and unkempt growth of hair on his face.

She headed down to the water, stopping when Cullan Donal knelt and with a stick made markings in the sand. He looked up at Martin and said something. His face looked tired from the exertion of walking all this way.

Cullan Donal made more marks in the sand, looked up and smiled at her son, then he looked in her direction. He stood and signaled for her to join them.

It would be a good time to talk to him about her son, who was still unmarried. If only she could get Cullan Donal alone. She had an idea.

"Morning lord," she said with a slight bow of her head. She turned to her son. "You have let your lord come out without his cloak on this cold morning," she scolded Martin. "Go back to his room and get it."

Martin looked at Cullan Donal. He smiled and nodded.

Mór watched as Martin made his way to the main gate.

"What is it I can help you with, Mór?"

"You have raised him well, but I am surprised that he is still unmarried."

Donal smiled. "There is a young girl, of good family that I hope he will like and that she will say yes."

At the sound of voices coming along the lake path, he dragged his sandal tip across what he had marked in the sand. She was surprised to see it was letters and numbers. Though she could both read and write she made no sense of what he had written there.

He stepped up into the trees.

Mór followed him. He did not want to be seen like this. Perhaps he had even heard the servants call him the Wild Man.

"I will come to your room after your evening meal and see to your hair and beard."

"I will be honored for your help," he said and bowed. "I see Martin has returned, if you will excuse me I will join him." He moved up though the trees. At the top he moved into the open. Martin waited for him at the far corner of the fortress. He helped Cullan Donal into his cloak. They turned and disappeared around the corner.

Mór as she had said, went to Cullan Donal's room to shave and cut his long mane of hair. She also had the servants bring a long tapestry-panel to partition off the back part of the room where she could see to his needs in private. Her servants had almost ruined the surprise with all their noise.

"What are they doing?" Cullan Donal asked.

"Preparing the water to wash your hair."

Mór combed out and cut his hair and shaved him so he now looked like the prince she remembered from her youth.

When she was done, she slid back the panel to reveal that the servants had brought up a tub and filled it with hot water.

Cullan Donal looked both pleased and embarrassed at the same time, knowing that she would have to help him into the bath. He looked relieved when Martin came in to help him.

∽

The next day, at the evening meal, Mór surveyed her domain. Her husband might be lord here, take care of the men and horses, the management of the land, but she saw to the running of the fortress. She was pleased when she saw Cullan Donal take his place next to her husband.

Unmarried women and even a few married ones looked in his direction, wondering if they had a chance with him. Even a few serving girls looked at him with desire in their eyes.

Cullan Donal was still a virile man.

Her thoughts went back to the morning before his wedding. She had found him in the chapel. As befitted a man about to be married.

She remembered his words.

"Do you think me an amadan for marrying so late in life?"

"A fool? You?" she said and shook her head. "Remember your ancestor Brian Mór was married in his seventies. And you are no where near his age."

Mór pulled herself to the present and glanced down the table at Cullan Donal. When a serving girl moved to refill his cup, he placed his hand over it. She was pleased to see her oldest son do the same.

Chapter Forty-One

One week before Samhain, Donal walked out of the main gate at Faolán. He moved down the incline to the loch. The lake had a thin coating of ice all around the edge, where the wind drove the water up higher on the rocky ground.

His arm was out of the sling, his hand was only immobilized now at night. Rónán gave him exercises to do everyday so the hand wouldn't stiffen up. Behind him he knew his two shadows followed. He liked Seta and Colm, but he was tired of walking the curtain wall, he wanted a quiet walk on his own.

Donal thought about his conversation with Rob earlier. At first his son had sat in the chair by his bed and stared at the floor, while Donal dressed for his walk.

Robert looked up. "I like Angel," he stammered.

"But not enough to stay?"

"Yeah, something like that. There is so much that I would miss."

"No problem Rob. I will send word to Feargus."

"Will she be all right?"

"There have been several inquires about her status. Feargus will find her a good husband. She has land and coin so he won't have any trouble there."

"How about Devlin?"

"I haven't seen him since the fight," Donal said. He had expected Devlin to come to Faolán. Where was Devlin? What excuse would he make to cover his absence when he returned?

"Lord Niall rode in late this afternoon, he is with Lord Rónán." Robert paused, "Da?"

"Yes?" Donal looked up from struggling one-handed with his boot, gave up and put on his sandals.

"When we were little, Donald and I found out where Martin and you practiced. We hid back in the trees and watched. I never thought I would see you actually put that practice to use, to have to fight a man. To..."

"I knew you were there."

"You knew!"

"Yes. Rón had found us sooner then you and your twin and was up in a tree watching. I never thought I would have to fight a man again, but I knew there was a good chance I would have to this time."

Donal cleared his head and turned away from the path to the village and walked up along the headland. He was cold, but it seemed to clear his head. His hair hung down just below his shoulders, his mustache was long and flowing as he had worn it in his youth.

He walked until he came to the highest point beyond Half Moon Bay. From here he had a panoramic view of the whole lake. To the west the sky turned a deeper blue, then purple streaked with red and gold.

Through the dusk he walked back to Faolán. He was surprised to see Niall and Martin coming out of the gate. Fionn followed leading two horses.

Niall stayed with his son.

Martin moved forward. "We are riding out tonight, so we will get to the Desert Pass during daylight."

Donal embraced his foster son. "May the Father keep you safe on your journey." Donal stepped back. "Remember if there is snow in the pass, come back."

Martin nodded, turned and walked back to the horses. Taking the reins from Fionn he mounted his horse. Niall embraced his son, Fionn, said a few private words to him before mounting his horse. The two young men rode around the castle to take the high road.

"We could walk to the village?" Niall said, as he joined Donal.

Donal shook his head.

"I know a place near by where we can talk."

Donal nodded, sent the brothers back to the fortress, and followed Niall.

In the woods not far from the lake they came upon a wooden structure. It was small, too small for a barn. Niall had brought a leather satchel with him. He opened the door, peered inside, and let Donal step in first. Niall ran his hand along the shelf by the door. He found a candle and flint, and tried to light it. Even out of the wind it took several tries before Niall managed to light the candle.

Donal looked around the small shed like building. Curraghs were stacked to the left of the door. The center was dominated by a wooden table and benches.

Niall placed the candle in a little wrought-iron holder in the center of the table. From his satchel he pulled a flagon and two horn cups. He tossed the satchel on the bench. "I did not think you would want to go to the village," he said, as he filled a cup and handed it to Donal, then filled one for himself. The two friends sat down on benches, across from each other.

Niall held up his cup, "To times without heartache."

"To peace, prosperity and good health," Donal said, and emptied his cup. The whiskey tasted wonderful. It burned a little, it brought moisture to his eyes.

"You have done much for my son. He looks well."

"I am proud to have Fionn as a foster son. I hope to find a wife for him in a few summers. After he comes back with Martin and we go to the fortress of Cwillan. I hope to arrange for him to spend time with Abbot Tuathall."

"Are they coming back? Martin and Fionn?"

"Yes, if the Desert Pass is still open they will," Donal said. "There is a chance that they will not be able to return before spring."

They talked a while about general things, things less important then what was on both their minds. Finally, Niall said, "I talked with your son, the healer."

Donal didn't asked about what. He wasn't sure he was ready for this conversation. Rónán probably asked Niall to talk to him.

"Your son says you spend the night wondering around the castle," Niall said.

"My bed is cold and unpleasant."

"Ask Mór, I am sure she would be happy to send a serving girl to warm your bed. From what I have heard, even one of her daughters would be happy for your company at night."

"I am sure Mór would," Donal said, and laughed. "But I love Moya and will not dishonor our marriage." he paused. "Though I had doubts at first, it was the right thing to do."

Donal fell silent. There was only the sound of the wind howling around the boat shed, as if trying to find a way in.

"Do you feel that the Father has righted something that should not have happened in the past?"

"Perhaps," Donal said. But sometimes he did feel that way.

"I knew a man who fell and from that time on he did not remember things that happened that very morning."

"And what did Rón say?"

"He said that Lun Dubh had hit you hard on the head with the flat of his sword."

Donal didn't comment. He sat deep in his own thoughts. Weeks had gone by without a memory of the time. He had what "modern doctors" on the other side of the portal called super autobiographical memory. He should be able to remember coming to Faolán. When he thought about it, in way he did remember coming here.

"Was I awake?" Donal asked

"You came in and out of sleep. In fact, Feargus thought the farrier had tried to kill you. I stepped in and put an end to that. Your last word was "Water." Your son, Rón, always seemed to know when you needed to get up, though they could not keep you awake.

"Feargus and I accompanied you here."

Donal held his cup out for a refill. This time he only sipped at the contents. Savoring the whiskey.

"I would not worry much about your memory. It was a blessing that they did not have to..." Niall paused.

"I know there was talk of cutting off my hand." Donal held up his hand, Rónán checked it each day. His hand was stiff, but it looked like he would not lose the use of it.

"It is better that you do not remember all the pain, and the pain of being moved."

Donal touched the silver brooch that held his cloak in place. "This is Feargus' brooch?"

"They wrapped you in a blanket to keep you warm. As they placed you in the wagon Feargus fixed it on the blanket so it would not slip off."

"Will I ever remember?" Donal asked his friend.

"Probably not. Do you remember the day your mother died?"

"Only what my uncle told me."

"Cullan Donal, it is for the best. Put this time behind you. You are growing stronger by the day. I understand that in the spring you will go home."

"Yes. We would have all gone home, but my son, Rón, thought it was best to come here."

Niall held out the flagon to refill Donal's cup.

For a second Donal hesitated, then he smiled and held out his cup.

CHAPTER FORTY-TWO

On Christmas Eve, Rónán sat with his brother Robert in the great hall of Faolán. Seta and Colm were sitting with them.

"Don't they ever relax?" Robert asked, watching Seta and Colm.

"They are father's personal guards, they take their duty serious."

Seta and Colm were eating. From time to time they glanced to the high table where Donal sat with Lord Rónán and guests invited to Faolán to celebrate the holy day. Donal would let the brothers finish their meal before he went back to his apartment, or weather permitting he walked the curtain wall.

Lord Rónán wanted Donal to stay longer than just until the spring, but his father wanted to go home. Donal missed Moya and his daughter, as much as Rónán missed Caitlín and also Siobhán. Funny he had played piano for her, what a dozen times or more? Still he missed her.

Next to him Robert sighed. His brother was impatient to get home.

"What has you so upset?"

"Nothing."

"Something must have?"

"I'm angry with Martin. I told him that if he went back early, that I wanted to go with him. He should have taken me, not Fionn. Instead, he sneaks out one evening and leaves me here."

"He looked for you the night he left. Where were you?" Rónán asked. Was Robert busy bedding one of the serving girls?

"After I talked to Donal, I went to the chapel."

Donal wouldn't be happy until Martin and Fionn returned. Now it looked like it wouldn't happen until spring.

"They don't even know when it is Christmas here," Robert said.

"They celebrate Christmas on the day that it had been celebrated under the Julian calendar. Some people call it Old Christmas. I thought you would be looking forward to seeing Aingeal soon," he said, hoping to change the subject. "Feargus is coming here sometime this week. I am sure he will have Aingeal with him."

"I'm not going to marry her. I told Donal."

Rón stared at his brother. This was interesting news. It came to him what was going on. "There is someone else?"

"Kind of, that is if I can repair some bridges." Robert's voice was slurred, from too much to drink.

Rón turned to Seta, "Has he been drinking long?"

"All day, lord," Seta replied.

Before Rón could question him further Donal joined them. Seta made to stand, Donal placed his hand on his shoulder forcing him to keep his seat.

Donal sat down. "Merry Christmas," he said in English. "Then wished the brothers Merry Christmas in their native language.

"I didn't know you celebrated Christmas," Robert said.

Rón braced himself, hoping that in his bad mood and with drinking too much, his brother didn't say anything stupid.

"Growing up we didn't do much at Christmas so I thought that you didn't believe in it."

"We received gifts," Rón said, hoping to head this off, as he aimed a kick under the table in Robert's direction and missed.

"What are you trying to say, Rob?"

"I didn't think you knew what Christmas was."

Seta and Colm looked up wondering what was going on. Rón shifted in his seat, uncomfortable with the way the conversation was going. Donal's hand on his wrist forced him to stay in his seat.

"You think I am a heathen, a pagan?" Donal finished for Robert.

"Da, don't listen to him, he has been in his cups all day."

Just as Donal looked like he was going to say more to Robert, one of Lord Rónán's men hurried into the hall. After talking to his lord, he hurried over to Donal. "There is a messenger from Cwillan, from our Ard Ri. Lord Rónán would like you to come to his council room to hear the message."

Seta and Colm followed Donal out of the hall.

Rónán turned to his brother, "Well, that went well."

CHAPTER FORTY-THREE

The winter days passed slowly for Donal and his sons and foster sons. The snow kept everyone inside by the fire. Only the sentries went out to take their place on the curtain wall.

Donal played Ficheall with Seta and Rón, or talked with Lord Rónán. Still the days dragged by for him. Some time after Imbolc, the festival that marked the beginning of spring, the weather turned milder. Not warm, but mild enough so that Donal could ride out to the meadows west of Faolán and get some fresh air and give Anfa badly needed exercise. The brothers, Seta and Colm rode out with him.

Half a moon later, Martin and Fionn returned.

"We made it back after Samhain, but the pass was closed. So we spent the winter with Vél at his holding," Martin said.

"When the weather lightened we checked the Desert Pass every morning, until we found the snow melted enough so we could cross the mountains," Fionn added.

Donal was pleased that they were back safe and sound.

"Moya, and Fionnuala, are they well?"

"They are," Martin said. "And very happy that you are well and will return in the spring."

"I miss them."

"Fionn, will you go see if you can get some ale," Martin said.

"Is there a problem?" Donal asked when they were alone.

"Devlin rode in just before we did."

"It is over time he joined us here."

"Please don't be mad. But the Ladies wanted you to have this," Martin said, as he pulled what look like a letter from the lining of his cloak.

Donal took the letter, slipped the plastic sleeve off, and threw it into the fire. He watched it burn before he opened the letter. Inside he found a photo of Moya, Fionnuala, and Caitlín, he held it at an angle so the firelight fell full on it. His daughter would be over a year old and perhaps talking by the time he returned, and Caitlín would be walking. It saddened him to think of the time missed with Moya and his two little girls.

He reminded himself, what he did here was important also.

He unfolded the letter.

Moya's writing wasn't the best, it was probably the first time she had to write something since she finished her studies as a young girl. She sent Donal her love, and went on about how much she missed him. He studied the photo again and then was about to throw both into the fire. He stopped, he should at least let Rónán see the photo before it was burned.

Donal turned to thank Martin. He was surprised to find that he was alone.

After his evening meal, Donal walked along the curtain wall. He stopped on the lakeside watching the end of day. He loved this land, he loved his home in the States too. But this was the land where he was born.

On his third trip around the wall he noticed someone leaning on the wall on the lakeside. As he approached Donal recognized Devlin.

He was about to tell Devlin he had expected him here at Faolán long ago, but before he had a chance. Devlin looked up. "Please forgive me. I was with our good abbot."

Donal waited.

"I am glad he is dead."

"Lun Dubh?"

"Yes. He beat me," Devlin stopped, shook his head. "I should start at the beginning."

"We could go to my apartment to talk."

"No, lord. It is better told here, in the dark for he was a dark person."

Donal signaled for Seta and Colm to move back.

"So tell me what happened," Donal said as he leaned on the wall next to his foster son.

"It happened twelve moons earlier, before I agreed to come with you. You have met my grandparents?"

Donal nodded, though not in years.

"I was seeing my grandmother and grandfather back to our family holding. On the road we met Lun Dubh, he offered to accompany us to the farm. I knew him as a man working to become a Guardian and welcomed his company."

Had he not heard any rumors about Lun Dubh?

"I see by your eyes, that you knew about him. I did not. It was at our farm that he had some problem at our small stable. But I still did not know."

Donal was getting a picture of why Devlin had come with him, why his brother wanted him safely away.

"It was on the road back that he offered to mentor me, to help me reach my goal of Guardian like my father. I was flattered; I thought him a great warrior…"

Donal waited.

"I did not know that he was no closer to his goal than I was. He wanted something more than friendship in return for his help. That price I could not pay. He beat me, and I was only saved because my brother came looking for me."

Devlin hung his head, sighed and looked up. "With the bad blood between us, Lonán convinced our father that it was time to honor his old pledge, and send me back with you."

"Ciarán did not know?"

"I made my brother promise not to tell."

"Do you love Aingeal?" Donal asked.

"Yes, with all my heart," Devlin said, without having to think about his answer.

"Then I will send word to Feargus that your obligation to me is paid, that there is nothing to stop you from marrying Aingeal."

"Cullan Donal, I do not know what to say."

"Then say nothing and get ready for your wedding day in the spring."

CHAPTER
FORTY-FOUR

In the spring Feargus sent his personal guard to escort Donal and his retinue to the fortress of Cwillan. At the gates, a young man, an aralt, came forward to speak to Donal. He rode a beautiful palomino horse in the old Irish way, with a head collar and a blue blanket with saffron fringe that almost reached the ground.

"I will go ahead and announce your arrival to our lord, and our people," the herald said.

"Please wait, I have someone to see before I go to the top," Donal told him.

The guards came to attention as their party rode through the gate. Donal was wearing a plain linen tunic over his leggings, the only adornment was the silver brooch on his cloak. He had hoped to enter the fortress without fanfare.

Everyone dismounted at the edge of the village and left their horses with the herald and two young boys with the promise of coins when they returned.

Donal hoped to go unnoticed, but with the size of the group with him it might be harder then he first thought. He would never be taken as just another visitor to the small village.

He walked down to the end.

Seta and Colm walked behind him, then came his sons and foster sons. Feargus' men brought up the rear.

Near the end of the village, he found the cottage with the blue door.

The world never stands still, there is always change.

The once small cottage with the blue door was larger now and had a slate roof. Where the old wooden stable once stood, a new stone building took its place, also with a slate roof. The boys hurling in front of the stable stopped to watch Donal, turned and called to someone inside. A stranger came to the door, seeing that they did not have horses he turned and disappeared inside.

At the forge a muscular young man, a stranger, worked on a pot while a young boy worked the bellows for him. The smith looked up, stopping with his hammer in mid air. "Can I help you, lord?"

Donal shook his head and started back to where they had left their horses. What had he expected? To see things as they once were.

They had only gone a dozen paces when Seta stopped and said, "Contúirt."

Donal turned to see what the problem was. The honor guard moved forward as an old man using a staff to walk hurried toward them shouting in a gruff voice for him to wait.

Martin moved up beside Donal.

The old man with a thatch of gray hair and scraggy beard stopped a few paces from Donal, unsure of himself. "Who says I am to take in another to feed and care for? These are hard times, I have enough of my own to see to.

The old man waited.

Donal smiled and replied, "I would rather sleep up in the loft."

The old man smiled, still not sure whether he should step forward or not.

"Baltice," Donal said, as he moved forward to embrace Ciarán's father.

"My son said he thought it was you. You have come for the wedding, then."

"I would not miss it."

"I hardly see Ciarán now, he is so busy. Émer and I live on the farm that Lonán lived on until his wife went to be with the Father. We care for his children." Baltice smiled, "It is good to see you again."

"It is good to see you also," Donal said. "Come meet my sons."

CHAPTER FORTY-FIVE

In his mind Donal heard the familiar voice again, *"You have to believe."*

He was sitting on a bench under the grape arbor in the Ladies Bower at Cwillan. Someone sat down next to him. He opened his eyes and smiled.

"You are too young to be sleeping in the sun," Ciarán said.

"Sometimes I feel very old."

"Sometimes when I see Lonán's or my brother's children I feel old. I am glad you can stay for the marriage."

Donal smiled, it would be an honor to see Devlin married.

"I thank you for your kindness in letting my son stay."

"I cannot stand between their love for each other. It is a good marriage, and I know Devlin will be a good husband. I will have to call him lord, he is now a landowner in his own right."

"He wishes nothing to change between you two. He says you have always treated him with respect."

"Niall trained Feargus well," Donal said, changing the subject.

"Feargus had faith that he could keep you safe. Faith and love are powerful emotions. He has raised the amount on Mangan's head, to catch him before he can make a new plan." Ciarán stood. "Your son, the healer is down in the practice field. Lord Rónán is trying to teach him how to use a sword. I would go down with you, but I must meet with our good abbot."

"Before I go," Donal said. "Before I return to my other home. The Four Horsemen will ride again, up into the White Mountains."

"As you wish."

೧౨

Donal watched Feargus spar with Rón. The practice swords were made of heavy wood to build up the arm and shoulder muscles. Lord Rónán coached Rón and Niall coached Feargus.

Feargus was taking it easy on his brother.

Donal watched for a while, before he went to look for Rob. It was time to settle their disagreement. He looked everywhere for his son. Not finding him, Donal went down to the kitchen thinking that his son might be there with one of his friends drinking.

He asked a serving girl. She pointed to one of the older red haired girls to ask.

The girl acted shy, as if she did not know why he was asking her, finally she blurted out the chapel, that Robert sometimes went to the chapel.

Donal paused at the heavy metal studded wooden door. He decided to go to the front. He opened the door and moved straight toward the high alter. He touched his forehead then his chest and was about to kneel when Rob's voice stopped him.

"Do you come here often?"

Donal turned, "Not often enough. Do you want some company?"

"Sure, why not."

Rob wasn't going to make this easy.

Donal sat down next to his son.

"Are you ready to go home?"

"Over ready. I would have gone with Martin if he had bothered to let me know he was going."

Was that the only problem?

"Are you going back to Boston right away?"

"Grandfather said that when I came back I would have a lot of things to straighten out. I need to think about going back to school. It was stupid of me to drop out. Then there is the matter of a friend."

They sat in silence for a while, before Robert spoke again.

"Do they crown the king here?"

"See the place about two thirds of the way up, where the stone shows more wear." The sun bathed the spot in slanting rays of spring sunlight, where dust motes danced.

"That is where generations of your forebears knelt, took their vows before the Father and Son and their chieftains.

In his mind, Donal was kneeling in tall grass, in a peaceful meadow. The dampness from the earth seeped through his leggings. Abbot Tuathall stood before him reciting the beliefs handed down for generations. They were the words of Déaglán, for his children, for his grandsons and granddaughters.

Niall placed the gold circlet on his brow and he stood.

"Interesting," Robert said. Pulling Donal back to the present. "I am sorry, I..."

Like Feargus, this was probably the closest to an apology that Donal would get from Rob.

"Why did Dearg have to cheat?"

"Over the years, his mother, or whoever raised him, fostered in him the kind of hate that blinds one to reason."

For a second Donal was in the room again with Taydan. He reached back and grabbed the wooden handle of the poker to defend himself with.

Donal cleared his head and went on. "Dearg agreed to end it if I won, but he wanted revenge. Honor meant nothing to him. He probably had it all worked out in his head what he would do if I won."

Robert brushed a tear away. He leaned forward, his hands laced together as if in prayer.

"You killed a man, son, but you also saved your brothers, Tuathall, Tole, and many others."

"I am not sure what I was thinking at the time, about you and Feargus I guess. I know I wasn't thinking about

Aingeal. The whole fight comes back to me in dreams. Sometimes at night...the whiskey and ale help...but..."

The door opened and Rón stuck his head in.

"Your archer friends and Fionn are downstairs. They have invited you to another competition."

"Go ahead, Rob."

Rón took Robert's place in the chapel.

"How are you feeling?"

Donal held up his hand, "Doing pretty good."

"No, I mean how are *you* doing?"

"I have a few things to resolve, then I'll be fine. Funny, earlier I was thinking about the rules I live by and here I am thinking of breaking another one of them."

"Have you talked to Tuathall?"

"I have."

"If it will help my brother or my people; I say go for it."

Donal smiled at his son.

"I might just do that."

"And Dad, I did the best I could setting the bones in your hand, the young farrier helped me, but make sure you get a specialist to look at it when we get home."

Donal nodded.

CHAPTER
FORTY-SIX

At the front of the chapel, Abbot Tuathall waited with Devlin. Donal stood to the left with Niall and Rónán, to the right stood Queen Niamh, Siobhán, and Mór.

In the audience were Ciarán's family, Donal's sons and foster sons. Also invited were the clan of Guardians. Usna stood with his three sons and Síle near the back.

It had been many years since Donal saw his former Guardian's mother, Émer and his brothers.

The years had been kind to Émer.

Baltice glanced in his direction and nodded. Donal smiled at him.

The door opened, Feargus, with Aingeal on his arm, stepped forward to escort her to the front. Feargus looked more like the groom than Devlin in his plain tunic and leggings. Feargus wore a linen tunic with gold and blue silk thread embroidered around the hem and neck, in an intertwining pattern; that In Donal's other home was called Celtic knot work. Aingeal wore a simple blue shift with a silk over gown and a short veil on her dark hair.

Niall leaned closer, "They would have made a stunning couple."

"I am sure Niamh will be happy to see her married and out of their lives."

Feargus moved over to stand next to Donal.

Tuathall had spoken with the young couple earlier, the bride's gifts were given at that time. He smiled at Devlin and gave him his vows. Then he spoke to Aingeal. Devlin placed a gold band with a heart engraved inside on Aingeal's finger.

"Is this a custom in your land?" Niall asked in a low voice.

"It is. I think it will become one here too. Feargus is going to give his queen a ring on the anniversary of their marriage," Donal whispered back.

The service almost over, "She is beautiful," Donal remarked, a little louder than he intended.

"Yes, she is," Feargus agreed. "More beautiful than a summer day, as enchanting as a rainbow, I give her my heart and my hand."

Donal turned, he had never heard Feargus recite poetry. He was pleased to find that his son wasn't looking at Aingeal, but at his queen across from them. Niamh watching the wedding, but sensing that someone was looking at her, she turned, smiled at her husband, blushed pink, and turned back to watch Devlin and Aingeal as they turned to the audience.

So, Niall was right, there was nothing between Feargus and Aingeal. It eased Donal's heart, one worry down and so many to go. But then that is how life went.

Now that the marriage celebration was over, the marriage contract would be read and the feasting would begin.

CHAPTER
FORTY-SEVEN

After they crossed the Glas River, the Four Horsemen; Donal, Ciarán, Lord Niall, and Lord Rónán camped for the night on the eastern bank. Feargus had sent an honor guard to accompany them. They made their own camp to the left, so the four friends would have privacy.

After their meal of fresh fish, caught earlier, they sat before the campfire talking.

"My son, Lonán, thinks we need more archers," Ciarán said.

Lord Rónán patted his sword, "Swordsmen are our best defense."

"He would also like to set up loyal men to the king," Ciarán said. "To work with the brehon to uphold the laws."

Donal listened to the argument going back and forth. Niall kept silent, watching Donal across the fire.

"And what do you think?" Niall asked, when his companions fell silent.

Donal had kept silent on purpose. He made his decision and said, "You are both right."

Ciarán and Lord Rónán looked at him, both seemed surprised at his comment.

"Déaglán, our ancestor, led a family clan, a small tribe, rather than a people that made up a country like those to the north or south of us. We are proud of our heritage. We have made this our home," Donal said. "But we hate change. Yet change comes whether we want it to or not."

"What are you trying to tell us?" Lord Rónán asked.

"The people to the far north and far south pick away at us. One day they will come with better weapons than ours to murder our children. We must be ready to adapt to their ways to defeat them. Listen to him," Donal paused, he was unsure how to put this. "Trust Lonán's ideas. Remember how well the archers worked for us at the Judgment Tree."

"We need to keep the other chieftains under control as well," Niall said.

"Yes, that is another important matter. Help Feargus to work toward that goal."

"I was pleased to see many of the southern lords stand with us at the Judgment Tree," Niall said.

"Yes, as was I," Donal said. "We also need to know which of the Lords betrayed Feargus and helped Mangan."

His friends agreed with him

Late the next morning, they reached the path that would take them up to the Silver Falls and from there up to the glade. Feargus' men would wait with the horses.

In daylight, the steps weren't as bad as Donal remembered. At the top the four friends stopped just inside the tree line, watching a doe with a fawn. The deer's head came up, ears pricked forward. She turned and darted off into the trees, the fawn hurrying to catch up.

Donal moved to the center of the glade, his companions followed. He turned his back to the place where he was sure the cottage had stood. Walking backwards he hoped to recapture the view he remembered as if in a dream, as he emerged from the cottage.

"It was here, I know it was here," Donal said and turned around. "And over there is were the bed stood."

Niall studied the area Donal indicated. "It is not here now. Nor is there any sign that one has ever been there."

"I'm not surprised that you do not believe me."

"On the contrary, I do. There are more things in heaven and our world than we mortals will ever understand. How else would you know the boy, Maiú, was really a girl. Plus there is the matter of your bandaged hand."

"And what is that?" Donal asked. "I though Usna bandaged my hand."

"I asked my son, Kenn, he did not want to say, but finally said Usna fixed your hand. So I went to Usna and asked him who had done it. He did not want to say either. But finally claimed he had."

Donal waited.

"Then I took Osisin Og to the horse pens. I had just bought a small horse. I placed him on the small horse; he loved the animal. Then, I asked who bandaged your hand."

Donal folded his arms across his chest and asked, "So, what did he say?"

"He hesitated. I told him that this would be between the two of us. He said that they found you sleeping among the rocks in a side canyon with your hand already bandaged."

Donal was surprised.

"I told him not to worry himself about it and gave him the small horse as a gift for finding your hair cord."

"I thought you were looking for a small horse for one of your grandchildren?" Rónán asked.

"I can find another."

Donal walked around the small clearing, nothing looked disturbed. It was strange that no new trees or bushes grew in the area where he was sure the cottage had stood. Niall was right, even his son who had befriended Síle had thought she was a boy.

"Perhaps it was an aingeal sent by the Father and Son?" Ciarán offered.

"If not an aingeal, perhaps someone from another world. The strange part about it is," Donal paused, "I think I have met her before."

"Give no more thought to it," Niall said.

Donal turned, and said to himself, "I believe," then followed his friend's back down.

◦◦

In a coffee shop in the suburbs of Chicago, Alvin and Michael O were talking in the back over cups of coffee. The bell over the door tinkled. Alvin looked up as a young lady came into the shop. She looked familiar.

"What's wrong?" Michael O asked.

"That girl at the counter," Alvin said, as he moved his chair so his back was to the front of the shop. "No, don't look. She looks familiar."

"Do you think you were followed?"

"No," Alvin said. "They aren't that smart. I am probably wrong. I don't think I know her."

◦◦

Out in the parking lot, two rows from the coffee shop. KC Little sat in his car waiting for Tracy to place the bug under the counter. While he waited he sent Seán Scanlon a message. He hoped help would get here in time to pick up Alvin and Michael O.

Tracy came out of the shop, took a sip of her coffee. After a slight nod of her head she turned right and walked along the storefronts to her car.

KC turned on the recording device and listened to the plans made by Alvin and Michael O.

❧

Uncomfortable, Alvin said, "Wait here, I am going to the men's room."

Instead of going into the men's room, he walked down the hall and out the door to the back parking lot. He hurried along the building. As he neared the corner, a car came around the building. He just had time to slip behind a dumpster. He recognized Seán Scanlon's car. It stopped behind the coffee shop.

Alvin waited until Cathal O'Brien and Seán Scanlon entered the back door. Alvin hurried to cross into the next parking lot, and down to the crossroad, turned left, and kept walking. When he was well away from the coffee shop he would see if he could find a cab.

It was unfortunate that Michael O had been caught. It meant he would have to find another person to help him.

CHAPTER
FORTY-EIGHT

At the Fortress of Cwillan, Robert asked again, "What does he want?"

"He has something he wants to give to Donal," Martin said.

"Why doesn't he just give it to him?"

"Come on Robert, we will be leaving this afternoon to meet dad in the foothills of the White Mountains. Let's get this over with," Rónán said.

Robert pulled on the neck of his tunic. "I'll be so happy to take a shower."

Martin agreed with him.

"I can't wait to to see Caitlín," Rónán added. "She will probably be walking by the time I get back."

They were admitted into the ante-room where private audiences were given.

Feargus and Lonán were playing chess. Feargus stood, Lonán remained frowning at the game board. Finally, he stood and picked up a wooden box with a circular interwoven pattern of running horses carved into the top and polished to a high gloss. He handed it to Feargus.

Martin leaned closer to Robert, "What ever you do don't ever play chess with him."

"Why?"

"Donal thinks he could beat the best of the chess champions."

Feargus addressed Rón. "This is for you and the Dark One to give to our father on his Naming Day."

Rón took the box. "May I look inside?"

Feargus nodded.

Robert and Martin moved closer so they could see. Inside was a book.

"It is a copy of *The Book of Dobrón*," Feargus said.

Martin looked up startled.

"The Book of Great Sorrow," Martin translated for Robert. "Started by Déaglán and finished later by one of his sons. Some believed its existence only a myth."

"Tell him to keep it safe. I placed a message for my father inside. I hope he will return to Cwillan soon. And when Robert returns, I hope that he has learned to speak our language."

Rón handed the box to Robert, who ran his hands over the top, feeling the fine finish. He smiled and bowed to his brother.

"Devlin will go with you to help with the young foal, a gift for my new sister, Fionnuala Mór, I sent it on to

Vél's holding. I will meet you below; then we can go to meet our father," Feargus said, dismissing them.

∽

It was a beautiful day, sunny. Above, small white clouds filled the sky, like a flock of sheep in a pasture of blue. As they walked down to the promenade, Martin and Robert discussed their audience with the king.

The group of archers that Robert had practiced with all winter were waiting to see him off. Also present were the four archers he had helped defend the Judgment Tree. Robert seemed both delighted and embarrassed at the same time.

Fionn translated for them. "They were honored to have you in their company and wish you well on your journey."

Each archer stepped forward and embraced Robert. "I don't understand." Robert said.

"Robert, you have become a folk hero, the battle at the lake will be told and retold for a long time. Perhaps you will become as famous as the Four Horsemen."

Robert bowed to the men. Seeing that Feargus was coming through the gate leading Lightning and Lonán leading his horse, the archers moved back.

Feargus mounted his stallion.

Lonán signaled for everyone to mount up. Once mounted Feargus' groom handed Rónán Donal's standard and he moved to the front to ride along side of Feargus' standard bearer. Next rode Feargus and Lonán,

Fionn, and Robert. Martin and Devlin rode ahead of six of Feargus' personal guards.

Robert smiled at Fionn, over the winter they had become friends. "You aren't coming back to Forest Lake."

"No," Fionn said. "I am going to stay here for six months to a year and study with Abbot Tuathall.

High above came the plaintive caw as a shadow fell over the riders. Everyone looked up, as the shadow turned and passed across their faces again. Then the raven wheeled off eastward.

Feargus whispered a prayer and touched his forehead, then his chest. All his men followed suit.

"Why would a raven cause such a response?" Robert asked.

"It is an omen," Fionn said. "For good or bad, I do not know."

⌒⌣

Donal and his friends and Feargus' men camped near a stream in the northern foothills of the White Mountains. After a quiet lunch they sat around the cook fire talking. Feargus' men camped a short distance away.

They talked of the summer to come.

Donal stood, stretched and signaled to Niall that he would be right back. He was impatient to get home. They were a day early, so they would have to wait for Feargus and his retinue to arrive.

Intending to go only as far as the water, Donal crossed the stream. The area was familiar to him. Less than a league beyond the woods was a hill and a good place to see if anyone was coming from the west. He climbed the hill, at the top he looked west. There was nothing moving on the great plains.

As he walked back down the hill his thoughts were of home. The gunshot snap of a breaking twig to his left pulled him out of his reverie. The hillside around him was silent, marred only by that one sound. Donal continued on his way as if he hadn't heard it. From somewhere behind him he heard another twig snap, then another to his right.

He was being stalked.

Donal whistled a tune, then did an up trill, then back down. When no answer came he knew his enemy had followed him and waited for their chance. If he could make it to the trees he might have a chance of losing them, or at least holding them off until they changed their minds.

He had made two grave mistakes. First, he had left his sword back at camp, and he had led Niall to think that he was going to relieve himself and would be back soon. How long before his friends came looking for him? Too long a time, far too long. All he had with him was his belt dagger. He kept his pace steady, but didn't hurry. He was almost to the tree line when the men moved in.

Donal, darted forward into the underbrush, ducking down and scrambling back into the shadows created by the trees.

"We should have stopped him before he made the trees."

"He could not have gone far. We will make a line of our men and flush him out as we come down through the trees."

Watching from the underbrush, Donal waited as half a dozen men moved across the hillside. Before they made their move, he made his. He gained the path and started his descent, giving no thought to the danger of his speed as he ran. He hoped that they had not sent men to bottom.

He zigzagged back and forth as the path allowed.

He ran up a hillock, from here the path below revealed the place where the trees thinned, from there it was less than half a league to the stream and safety. He started down, congratulating himself on his success, when a man carrying a club stepped from the trees at the bottom of the path.

Donal slowed, before he sped up. He had one chance, and only one. It was now or never as he ran toward the man as fast as his legs would carry him.

FAMILY TREE

<u>Déaglán</u> - had four sons and three daughters: Áedán, Keegan, Fintan, Cuilin, Síle, Aine, Caitlín.

<u>Cullan Donal</u> - is from the line of Déaglán's oldest son, Áedán, who married one of Brian Mór's daughters.

<u>Donal Tolan</u> - (Cullan Donal) with Aoife, had a son, Feargus. By Cynthia Long he had twins, Robert and Donald, and Rónán. He had one child with Moya, Fionnuala Mór.

<u>Rónán Tolan</u> had a daughter with Jennifer Strickland named Caitlín Aine.

<u>Cuilin</u> - Déaglán's youngest son, was lost in the Great Desert.

<u>Mánus Seamus Scanlon</u> - is from the line of Déaglán's third son, Fintan.

<u>Brid</u> - is from the line of Déaglán's third daughter, Caitlín.

<u>Liam O'Brien</u> - is from the line of Brian Mór

<u>Keegan</u> - was said to have gone west

GLOSSARY I PEOPLE

Áedán	- oldest son of Déaglán
Alvin O'Brien	- youngest son of Cathal
Aoife	- Second wife - Cullan Donal
Artúr	- Kin of Cullan
Beon	- youngest son of Vél
Brian Mór	- Brian the Great - Brian Boru
Brid	- fortune teller
Briana	- first wife of Cullan Donal
Caitlín	- Rónán's daughter
Callie Weston	- security with MSS

Ciarán	- Donal's former Guardian, now Feargus' Guardian
Colm	- younger brother of Seta
Cullan Donal	- Donal Cullan Tolan
Cuilin	- Déaglán youngest son
Cynthia Long	- Donal's third wife
Darlisca	- warlord from the north
Déaglán	- Leader of his clan
Dearg	- son of Taydan
Devlin	- youngest son of Ciarán
Donald Tolan	- Donal's youngest twin
Feargus	- Ard Ri of Cwillan
Fionnuala Mór	- Donal's daughter
Fintan	- Feargus oldest son
Fionnbar	- Fionn, youngest son of Lord Niall
Lun Dubh	- tracker

Maiú   - Sile pretending to be a village boy

Mánus Scanlon   - Donal's partner

Michael O   - Michael O'Brien

Kleeta   - Lord of Tir Lú

Riga   - Story teller

Ruadrí   - one of Feargus' men

Rhyianna   - Brid's daughter

Rónán Tolan   - Donal's son, Rón

Robert Long   - Cynthia Tolan's father

Robert Tolan   - Donal's oldest twin

Seta   - oldest of the Brothers

Vél   - friend of Donal, Horsemen

GLOSSARY 2
PLACES AND
WORD MEANINGS

Airgead	- silver
Athair	- father
Aralt	- herald
ard fheis	- (ard desh) High assembly
Ard Ri	- High King
cuaird	- visit
eíst	- Listen

Faolán	- fortress and Lake
Fásach	- desert
Mo ghrá	- my love (grá)
Mór	- great
púca	- horse spirit, ghost
reachtaire	- steward
Samhain	- Summers End
Tinreach	- lightning, Feargus horse
TOSE	- Tolan, O'Brien, Scanlon Enterprise
uisce bheatha	- water of life
Wyneth	- land west of Cwillan

Many Thanks

To Ken Gangwer and Rosemary in Ireland.
Without their help this book would never have
been possible.
Many thanks to my editor, Heather Murray.

And for Fred P. Wessells, you are missed.

To my father, who gave me the chance and
the opportunity to write this book.

To the real Donal Tolan and Mánus Scanlon,
May the Father and Son keep you safe.
May you never lose your Celtic Soul

Cover Photograph By
Celtic Cat Photos
www.etsy.com/shop/Celticcatphotos